I Thought I Was Alone

TRILOGY

I0628282

MIRIKA MAYO CORNELIUS

author of Inside the Gates of Doons, Disguised by a Raging Smile and The Secret Novel Collection

I Thought I Was Alone Trilogy

I Thought I Was Alone Trilogy

An Akirim Press Publishing
Book Cover by Akirim Press/Rod Cornelius
www.akirimpress.com

I Thought I Was Alone Trilogy

<u>Acknowledgements</u>

I first and always thank God for the giving of his Son, Jesus, to save me, and I acknowledge and confess that without Him, I have and am nothing.

To my family, I love you all. Mom, you're one special lady, dad and step-dad – you are awesome in unique ways.
Brothers and sisters, nieces, nephews, uncles, aunts, cousins, friends and fans who are like family…you rock. Always love.

To all in my family who have gone to our heavenly home, I love you still.

To my son, you are my heart. I cherish you as the special gift sent from our Father in Heaven. You make me better, and I love you. To my husband, we did it again. Love you.

mirikacornelius.com

I Thought I Was Alone Trilogy

I Thought I Was Alone TRILOGY

There's nothing more terrifying than being stalked by the unknown, sucked in by something or someone strange, and smitten by the slaughtered, and all of this comes inside the I Thought I Was Alone Trilogy.

I Thought I Was Alone

Trina secretly throws a big house party at her parents' six bedroom home while they are out of town. Things at the party are fired up, with partygoers stretched from wall to wall, until the party comes to an abrupt end. Trina believes that everyone has left for the night, but she soon discovers that not everyone has left her home.

There is someone still there.

Her life takes a deadly turn, putting her at odds with a deranged stranger who just won't leave her house or her alone!

I Thought I Was Alone 2

When you're out with your friends, he's watching you.

When you're asleep, he's watching you.

When you're alone, he's there.

Ayana has just arrived to college and is on top of the world, but something just isn't right. She feels like someone is stalking her, watching her, waiting to attack her. Then she finds out that… she's right.

I Thought I Was Alone 3

Charlotte and Tyrese appear to have a picture perfect marriage with promising careers and a nice home, but when Tyrese finds himself in a deadly situation that could potentially wreck everything he and his wife have built, he soon discovers that every single step he takes, he isn't taking alone. Someone is watching his every move and waiting for the perfect moment to turn his life, and the lives of those around him, into a nightmare. It should be no surprise when Trina enters the fold searching for answers about her past that bodies start dropping!

Follow the terrifying footsteps of Charlotte, Tyrese, and Trina in this final installment of I Thought I Was Alone!

Table of Contents

I Thought I Was Alone Trilogy

I Thought I Was Alone

"No, yeah…come on over, Grace. I've already started getting ready, plus I need some company to ride with me and get the food for tonight. I thought I'd save some money by opting to pick it up myself," explained Trina on speaker phone as she plugged the brand new floral scented air fresheners into the walls of the living, dining and entertainment rooms.

"Are you sure this is gonna go down like you planned? You know how your dad is with popping up or at least sending someone to pop in and check on you."

"No, seriously, Grace, you worry too much," Trina continued, pulling back from plugging in the last air freshener so that she could freshen up her own look in the elongated mirror that hung right outside of the guest bathroom. "Everything is going to be perfect. He told me that he would have Jeremy check on me, but listen to this…he lied. Jeremy can't go anywhere because running that ball up and down the football field got his ankle busted once again, and according to his little sister, the doctor ordered him down. On top of that, he isn't even back in town from college tonight. Word is, he'll be in town tomorrow, and that will be long after this particular party is officially over. So listen, I've been planning this for two weeks, therefore, I need you to be my backbone for this fantastic party and not my brain bone."

"And what's that supposed to mean, Trina? Brains don't have bones. They look like coiled diarrhea," she laughed.

"What it means is to not over think my dad crashing this party somehow," Trina sang. "Stop thinking about all the bad that could happen and soak up all the fun you are about to have right here with me." She waltzed away from the mirror about to grab her purse from off the stand beside the front door. "I hope you're on your way because I have to go get this food and…"

"I'm already here," Grace responded as she stood next to Trina's red sports car, watching her open the front door.

Trina stood there, shook her head, tossed her cell phone into her purse, and walked down the steps of the two, story six bedroom four bathroom, triple car garage home, with a basement

13

apartment that was worth anyone's while if they came to visit. Until then, it was her dad's man cave.

"Well, we aren't taking that one," she responded, referencing the red sports car. "Hop in the SUV since you're already here so we can ride out," Trina stated while hitting the alarm so Grace could get in. "You always have jokes. You could've told me that you were standing outside."

"Good ones," Grace responded as she locked her car doors and hopped into Trina's SUV. "I only have good jokes. I hope you brought a snack for me," she continued as she shut the door. When Trina got behind the wheel she answered.

"I always have snacks." At that, she popped open the glove compartment. "Take your pick."

There were gummies all over, from the worms and bears to even the soda shaped gummies. Trina also had crackers and a bottled water somehow stuffed inside the small compartment, however, when she looked under the armrest, Grace saw more.

"Dang, girl. How often do you eat, and why don't you gain any weight? Are you one of those binge eaters and the next thing you know is you're off to the bathroom to vomit to hell. Is that you?"

"Grace, do you see what I mean? You need to calm down," she responded, backing the car out of the semicircle driveway. "That crap isn't even funny. You know I had a cousin with that disorder."

"No…my bad. I'm sorry…but I wasn't trying to be funny. I was dead serious. I mean, who rides around with all this food hidden?"

"I'm not hiding it. I just have it…as long as my mom doesn't find out," she laughed. "Look, I'm almost grown, and she still tosses out my candy every second she gets. It's almost like she's a damn dental hygienist. She's so anal about it all, but that's why I'm glad they're both gone. I can finally be me…once again."

"And we are two of a kind!" Grace laughed as they slapped pinky fingers. "Check this out." Grace leaned over and slid out two mini bottles of alcohol, waving them in the air.

"Girl, put that stuff down. You see us driving down the road. Are you nuts? The cops will pull us over in no time, and you should have told me you had that stuff in your purse. What if I get stopped?"

"You don't have it. I do," she said tucking the bottles back in. "That will give everyone the extra buzz they need…take the edge off for us and them." Trina rolled her eyes, but Grace caught her mid roll. "Don't worry. It's not enough to get anyone drunk. They'll drive home just fine. It's not like half of them aren't coming with the bottom of the bottle already downed anyway, Trina."

"Yeah well, I just want to have fun, not get anyone killed or hurt or on punishment for life behind being drunk…not by me. If they come drunk, then hey. They didn't get it from me. That's all I want to know."

After chatting about the party for fifteen more minutes down the road, they arrived at the grocery store to pay for the catered sandwiches, deviled-eggs, cakes and deserts for the guests that were due to arrive at ten o'clock that night. The bakery was in the process of finishing one of the cakes, therefore, Grace ran to grab an additional shopping cart in order to get some extra sodas and chips for the long night they planned on having. As she wheeled the shopping cart, she halted suddenly as she stared down the soda and snacks aisle.

"Oh shit," she stated, then she immediately moved the shopping cart over to allow an elderly lady by who was obviously struggling with her cane and wheeling at the same time. "Ma'am, do you need some help?" she asked the lady, still glancing back down the aisle at the young man standing there sorting through the clearance chips that were piled into a huge barrel dead center of the walkway.

"Oh thank you, sweetheart. I need to get the box of noodles from the top shelf if you don't mind."

"Sure, sure…no problem. I'll grab a couple of them for you. How about that?" she continued with a smile. The elderly lady nodded her head, thanked her and then placed her cane inside the shopping cart. From there, she went on her way as Grace fixed up her clothes, took a second peep at the young man still pondering over the chips, and scooted quickly back to Trina.

"Girl!"

"What's up?" Trina asked appearing annoyed at the long wait for the cake.

"Guess who's in here, like right now?" Grace asked, gripping the shopping cart like she just won the lottery which caught Trina's attention immediately.

"Don't lie," Trina ordered, staring Grace square in her eyes that were lined with a thick rug of eyeliner and fake lashes that resembled windshield wipers. "Do not freaking lie, Grace, or I swear I will embarrass the hell out of you right here, right now."

"It's Creed!" She then lowered her tone and scooted in closer to Trina whose face was filling with disbelief. "Creed, Creed, Creed!" she repeated. "I saw him in the snack aisle. You know how he likes those chips, girl, and who I saw wasn't a mistake."

"Oh my gosh, Grace. You're serious, aren't you?" Trina turned around to hide her face from anyone who walked from the aisles. Then, Grace twisted her arm, causing her to turn back around.

"Go talk to him," she urged Trina, tossing her hands up in the air in frustration. "You've been wanting to talk to him, so go…now! You haven't seen him since…I don't know how long."

"I broke up with him when he went away though, Grace. What if he has another girl…friend?" she pondered, struggling with the thought of it all.

"Who cares?" she shrugged with a smile. "Take his fine ass from her. You know he still loves you…and look at you." She eyed her blushing friend who fiddled with her freshly done hair while shaking out her wrecked nerves. "You're still in love with him, too. You better go ahead before I step to him to see if I'm his type yet."

"Okay, okay, stupid. Back up. The snack aisle?"

"Yeah…and I'll wait here on this cake. And, Trina," she called, grabbing her at the end of her shirt. "Invite him to the party. You know, catch up while your parents are away."

Trina didn't answer, but instead, gathered the courage that she believed she didn't have enough of only five seconds ago. Then, she walked nervously toward the snack aisle. As she passed the shoppers, she hesitated as doubt crept up on her like a silent assassin, but before she even turned the corner, Creed walked directly in front of her. She paused, and as he turned to walk toward the register, she spoke.

"Creed…Creed, turn around." She placed her hands into her back pockets as she rocked back and forth on her tip toes. Her heart pumped extra beats as she finally was able to take another look at him, and as soon as she saw his face, she fell deeper in love.

When he turned around to face her, he didn't say her name. Instead, he tossed the chips onto a stand, stood there and then looked around the store. Finally, his eyes landed to a place somewhere beyond the exit, and he reached out for her hand.

"Let me talk to you for a minute."

Without a second thought, Trina's hand was inside his, and she was being led out of the store while Grace watched from the sidelines. Trina refused to look back at her because she felt the jitters already. It had been a whole four months since she'd seen Creed or even spoke to him at all. He was barred from calling her house, and her parents would periodically check the incoming and outgoing calls on her cell phone to make certain that he wasn't on the other end of any of the calls. Creed was the type of person people would call a bad boy, but he was good to Trina - always had been and always promised that he would be.

As they escaped to the outside of the store, Creed walked her only a couple of steps from where shoppers were entering and exiting. This was typical of Creed, not giving too much insight into what people thought about what he said or did in his life. Whatever it was that he did, it was always with his full heart, and he never apologized for it.

"Stop looking over at them," he said, referring to the shoppers as he noticed Trina glancing at them while he stared into her brown eyes. "They don't mean anything. They don't even know us, Trina, so..."

"Not even a hi, Creed?" she asked as she finally looked back at him, causing him to smile. Then, he leaned in and kissed her, and because she couldn't help it no matter how hard she tried not to do so, she kissed him back. The feeling of Creed on her skin again made her feel protected and secure, like a girl in love should feel with her man.

"Not even a happy birthday, Trina?" he asked as he pulled away from her lips softly.

"Happy birthday."

"Did you forget already?" he asked as his piercing blue eyes drained the power from her steady gaze, causing her to reach in to rub the back of his neck and up in to his soft dark brown hair while she kissed him again.

"No, I didn't forget. I didn't even know you were out. I'm sorry about how I..."

18

"I already forgave you. Don't worry about that shit, Trina. I never held anything against you, and I never will. Shit happens." He softly rubbed her flawless brown skin as he leaned in and kissed her forehead right at her hairline. "I went to jail for a minute, so how is your dad supposed to like me, right? I understand the man, so let it go." He looked over at the exit to only spot Grace walking out with a cart full of food, and when Grace spotted them talking on the brick wall, she shouted.

"You owe me. I just paid for all this food right here since you were tied up...," she paused. "Well, hello, Creed! I didn't know you were out... here," she added and lied.

"Sure you didn't," he answered sarcastically, "What's all the food for?"

"The party that Trina's having tonight. Trina, you didn't tell him?"

"I didn't have a chance to yet, but he's coming. Aren't you, babe?" she asked sure of herself as she admired his strong jaw bone and the muscular cut he didn't lose when he was locked up.

"Anything you want. Hey, Grace, what you say if I call Trina on your phone today? Are you gonna be with her all day?" he asked to evade Trina's parents' prying eyes on the cell phone log.

"Sure. Hit me up. Do you still have my number?"

"Yeah, I got your number." He looked back at his ex with a relieved smile on his face. "Are you still mine in these streets, or do I have to move the new man over?"

"I wouldn't be out here with you, Creed, if I didn't still love you," she reassured him softly. "If I was with someone else, at this point, I'm not anymore."

"I love you, too." He kissed her on her neck as he enjoyed the scent of her skin. She'd worn nothing but his favorite perfume since he'd been locked away for an assault that he finished. No one knew who started it, however. "I'll be there. Pops must not be home. What time?"

"Ten. Be there at ten…no nine-thirty. I want some time alone with you."

"You bet. Thanks, Grace," he said, walking over to her and handing her the money for the food. "That's for Trina." Then, he walked back into the store, and Grace hustled over to her friend who was left in a dream world.

"Well, he's the same old Creed, and you're just like a real piece of chocolate to melt inside his mouth and hands."

"Shut up, Grace," she laughed. "I missed him," she sang, "so much. You just don't know."

"Yes I do…with his fine, white ass. That's the finest white boy I have ever seen in my life. I swear he's black underneath all that fineness. You better hold onto him tight."

Trina looked back at the grocery store sliding doors as they walked across the street to her car. "I don't have to hold on tight. Not at all. He's not going anywhere, and I'm not either."

***

"You see how fine your man has gotten behind bars, girl?" Grace asked while lifting two trays of fruit from the back of the SUV. "It looks to me like you need to send him back for touch ups every once in a while. Creed has never looked…"

"Uhm…excuse me, Grace," Trina interrupted, slamming her door with a slight grin on her face while rolling her eyes at Grace as she grabbed the bottles of soda. "Don't be looking at my man. Go get yourself one. As a matter of fact, his dad's single now. Go for it because they look just alike."

20

"Bye, Trina, really? I don't date anyone six years older than me, and that's that. Unless he is twenty-three or younger, dad can hit the curb."

Trina grinned again, and they both walked up the stairs and into the house. As Grace ran back outside to gather the rest of the food, Trina started setting up the long, rectangular tables that were to hold the refreshments. She began to feel uneasy that Creed was coming to the party. Although she'd invited him, she didn't fully think the whole thing through. Suddenly, she left the refreshment table and walked back over to the mirror that hung at the side of the guest bathroom. She then turned to the side, staring hard at her size.

"Well, are you gonna help me or what?" Grace complained, hauling two more trays in her hand with a bag in the other. "If I would have known you were gonna be standing in the mirror all smiles, I would've sat my ass down to relax, too."

"My bad, Grace. I'm just nervous, that's all," Trina sighed as she rushed to the door to help her with the food. As she took the trays from Grace's hand, she appeared like she was in another world.

"What's wrong with you? You look like you've seen a ghost, and I don't do haunted houses. If someone died in here anytime in the last two weeks," she continued as she stepped into the kitchen, placing the bag on the counter, "you need to let me know."

"No, it's nothing like that. I just..." she paused, glancing up at Grace from the side of her eye while putting the sandwich trays on the counter next to the microwave.

"What?" Grace encouraged her friend as she freely opened the stainless steel refrigerator. "Oh look, this is just what I need in my life. Can I swallow a couple?" She removed the transparent, plastic bowl that was half filled with strawberries.

"Sure," Trina stated as she collapsed her body onto the table.

"Well? What's wrong? Don't let my smacking stop you," Grace stated, popping a strawberry in her mouth.

Trina watched her chewing but chose to wait until she took the first swallow before she answered. "I kinda had a baby."

The sink was right beside Grace thankfully because she'd just bitten down on the other half of the strawberry when she completely spit it out. It landed in the proper place. Her eyes bulged from her head, and she slammed the bowl of strawberries on the counter before walking to the table to have a seat. Everything was quiet as Grace stared at her motionless and Trina stared back without much more to say. Then, Grace turned her head toward the direction of where the guest bathroom was and then back at Trina, obviously putting pieces of the puzzle together as her mouth filled with dryness from it being open for so long. Finally, her mouth shut, but then it opened again so that she could speak.

"What do you mean, you had a baby?" The hair from her long ponytail extension draped her shoulder, but at that particular point, it annoyed her. Therefore, she whipped it back from so that it landed on her back while she continued to gawk endlessly at a fidgeting Trina who took two steps away from the table.

"I mean, I had one. I don't have it anymore," she stated clearly holding back an emotion that Grace didn't understand. "It was Creed's."

"Hell no, stop lying, and it ain't April," Grace responded quickly and through her teeth. She then walked toward Trina who looked like she was about to cry. "You're serious, aren't you?" Grace then looked down at her stomach. "Is that why you were putting on a little bit of weight like…a month ago?"

"It wasn't that much, but it was enough that I had to take care of it. I knew when it happened, but I didn't say anything to him about it. I thought maybe…"

"Maybe what?" Grace interjected, but her cell phone rang. "Hello?" she answered without even looking at the caller ID, but when she heard the voice on the other end, she just handed the phone to Trina. "Creed." Then, she sat back at the table, shaking her head and watching Trina talk...which is why Trina turned and walked down the hall.

"Hey, baby," Trina stated as she tried to calm down from the conversation. Her throat felt inflated because just speaking to him immediately after thinking about what she had done to their child made her feel terrible. After he went away, she didn't realize that her feelings for him would remain as strong as they had...even through their child being gone.

"Hey, baby? I missed talkin' to you. Most of my time in there, I didn't call anybody. Just thought about you, Trina, so seeing you today was a birthday treat all in itself. How have you *really* been?" he asked, sounding more settled than he was earlier at the store, desiring a more private conversation.

Trina walked into the bathroom and sat on the edge of the sink as she replied with her head held down and eyes closed in an attempt to block out everything she had going on in order to focus solely on their conversation

"I've been good...really good. I was about to tell you before you cut me off at the store that I'm sorry for breaking up with you. I still love you, and it was a mistake. I made a mistake, and I haven't been with anyone else," she paused, "because I don't want anyone else."

Trina's emotions shifted from sadness to a deep yearning to be in Creed's arms. She felt it amazing how a man, who could obviously be with anyone he wanted, forgave her and understood her parents, all at the same time. To Trina, Creed may not have been the most law abiding citizen at all times, but he understood something that most people didn't – life. He knew how to live it, make it, and keep going, including take care of what she needed the most – attention and love.

Creed had loved her more than any other boy, but it was unfair to compare any boy to Creed because he had much more independence and could do more for her than any school aged boy.

Even though Trina was accustomed to having money and Creed didn't have half of what her parents did, everything he had was somehow worth more to her. She felt like any five dollars he had, he really worked for it, so it had more leverage than the five dollars that she would routinely find in the dryer or even the trashcan from her parents misplacing it. Trina would always snatch them up and add the trace dollars to her collection which made for so much extra in her allowance.

"You know how to make a man feel like he's worth something, baby. I love you, too, and that was all on me. I shouldn't have gotten myself locked away like that because it's gonna hurt me in the long run."

"It won't hurt you, Creed. You'll turn it all around. I know you will because you always do," she stated as she turned to face the mirror. "When you get over here, I need you to come upstairs with me to talk really quick about something before the people get here."

"We gonna do more than talk, huh? It's been too long, T, baby."

"No seriously, we do have to talk, so get here…at nine-thirty sharp," she sighed. "I gotta go…"

"What is it?" he cut her off, his voice sounding less calm than when he called.

"Just get here, okay? I love you," she said as she slumped over and left the bathroom in worse emotional shape than she came. She'd just asked Creed to talk to her about the one thing she didn't know if she could even say when she ended up facing him before the party.

She turned around and began to leave the bathroom with thoughts about how the only person she'd told was her mother. Trina became panicked and ended up telling her about the pregnancy, but it became the perfect blackmail. Her mom told her that she could avoid the situation by getting an abortion, she would even pay for it, but she had to break up with Creed and never see him again. The only other option she had was to have the baby and get out of the house along with it. Her mom wasn't about to have any parts of Creed living in the house, and that meant the baby.

Out of fear, Trina chose the route that her mother paid for and what her mom considered would give her better options in life, but now that she and Creed were back together, she would have gone back on her word. Trina had no other choice. She wanted to be the first person to tell Creed about the abortion. If her mother found out that they were back together, she would go above and beyond to let him know. That information would destroy any future Trina had with Creed, so she had to tell him. The truth coming from her own lips would block any other form of blackmail or damage from anyone outside of their relationship.

As Trina walked back to the kitchen, she met Grace who was still sitting there anxiously awaiting the details of the conversation. She tossed the cell phone back to Grace who leaped forward to catch it in mid air.

"Girl, don't toss my phone. Does my body look like I run up and down a field playing football?" she complained as she sat back into her chair as she checked the face of her phone. Then, she looked back at Trina who was just standing there like her world crumbled. "So did you tell him?"

"No…I couldn't. I just told him I would tell him when he got here," she sighed, "so could you do me a favor and cover for me as the people start coming in. You know this house just as well as I do so…just in case when I tell him, I end up sort of away for a little while."

"Yeah…you may be in there for a while, Trina, with news like that," she stated, standing up from her seat. "But you need to tell him, so woman up."

They both walked back to the entertainment room, and on the way back they talked more about the party and even more about the abortion. Trina ended up feeling good about finally telling Grace all about it because she made her feel like she made the right decision. She just hoped Creed felt the exact same way.

***

As she stared out of her window looking for any sign of Creed who hadn't showed to the party when she expected, she watched the crowd of partygoers gather into her yard. The cars lined not only her driveway but continued to take up both sides of the road. When she noticed people being dropped off that she didn't even recognize, she became annoyed.

"Damn," she sighed, leaving the window and moving over to her closet mirror. "I didn't want the whole damn city partying at my place," she complained, still not understanding why Creed hadn't showed up.

Her long, golden earrings dangled beyond her shoulders, and she wore a highly elevated ponytail which accented her ear garb, neck and shoulders as she wore a loose, sleeveless, pink V-Neck blouse that fell open to right above her navel to meet the ripped blue jean, skin tight short shorts she had on just for Creed. He loved her legs. Her feet were pumped with wedged heels, and as she twirled one last time in the mirror, she set off downstairs, locking her room door behind her as she did all the upstairs rooms.

"Creed, please be down here," she sighed as she went step by step down into the party. Everyone noticed her as she made what she didn't mean to be a grand entrance.

Trina fluffed out her blouse and scanned the crowd before her feet hit the hardwoods of the spaciously open home. Creed was nowhere to be found, but in her heart of hearts, she knew that he was coming. He may have been late a few times, but Creed was never one to stand her up...and she was right. As she turned to face the front door, there he was just walking inside. Trina immediately made her way to him as he stood there against the front door's entrance taking the last puff from his cigarette. He looked relaxed as he paid no attention to the people stepping over him to walk inside. That was the thing about Creed that Trina admired – his confidence. He always lived in the moment with no fear, and he always handled things one step at a time, never in a rush. Nothing, not even a crowd of rowdy people, created a stir in him or made him another type of man. He was the same, love him or hate him, and Trina was in love.

Trina moved around the crowd quickly, even hearing some people call her name, but she ignored them. She saw Grace to her right looking at her with her thumbs up in the air, and she knew that meant that she had everything under control. Therefore, she continued toward the man whom she missed so much, and when she reached him, she placed her hand inside his pocket as she would always do, and he turned to face her.

"Hey, baby." He leaned in to kiss her on her neck as he always would and on his way back up, she would place the second kiss on his lips.

"Hey," she responded back. "Why didn't you let me know you were out here. I've been upstairs waiting."

"I just got here. I ditched my car down the road back there. Look at all these people, babe. Nobody else can drive up here without getting into a wreck, so I apologize for getting here late."

"Hey, Trina, girl! Your house is nice," squealed a female partygoer that had already doubled up on the food.

"Yeah, thanks. Leave room for the pizza that's coming," Trina smiled back as she turned her back to Creed and laid back into his arms. When his arms locked around her stomach, every thought of his baby came to her memory, causing her to tense up. Creed felt her discomfort.

"It's just my hands, baby. What's going on? They feel different or something?" he laughed.

She quickly turned around and took him by his hands. "No, it's nothing like that. You know I like to feel you touching me, but I just needed to talk to you…"

He looked inside the house at everyone and then back at Trina. "Let's go have some fun first. We got all night, right? You didn't throw this party on my birthday for nothing. I know you better than that."

Trina turned back to look inside at the swarm of people, and then back at Creed. "You're right, I didn't. It was the only way I could celebrate you without actually having you here with me."

"Well, you got me now, babe," he assured her, kissing her once again on her lips. "Let's celebrate."

After feeling just how tense she was getting just thinking about the weight of information she had to relay to him, she felt the need to let it all go for another day. The night really shouldn't have been spent dwelling on all the bad when Creed was out and in her life again, and to top it all off, it was on his birthday. The night couldn't have been any better, so she was going to have some fun.

"You know what? You're absolutely right. It's your birthday weekend so let's get this party started the right way," she said pulling him by his hand and dragging him inside the house amongst the crowd. Then she yelled out loud while Creed started greeting people that he hadn't seen in a long time, "Everybody listen up! If we're gonna party, let's party right! Turn the music up! My man is back home, and it's his birthday so turn up! Grace, you know what to do."

Grace rushed from her spot to see a happy Trina still in her right mind, so she went over to the punch and spiked it, as she assumed that's what Trina wanted. She was right. Like a lightning bolt, Trina made her way to the table while Creed followed behind much slower, becoming overtaken with pats on the back and shouts that were of the happy birthday kind.

"I thought you and Creed broke up, Trina, baby," said one guy walking up to her as if he didn't see Creed only three or four steps behind.

"Well," Trina stated with a smirk, "I'm always one for surprises. Do I even know you?" she stated, turning away from him purposely closing her ears to any answer he had to give. Although he was ignored, he took a quick glance at Creed and then back at Trina as she walked away. He then spoke.

"You can get to know me, Creed or no Creed."

"I don't hate the playa, man. I don't," Creed stated walking up toward him, catching his name sailing from the unknown guy's lips. "I just hate the playa who is going after my lady right there." Creed glanced back at Trina and then back into the male's face. "You want some?" Creed asked calm and collected because he knew the pinned up aggression he had from spending time in jail all those weeks, and the one thing he needed was a reason to release it all.

The guy, who stood about one to two feet taller than Creed, started to grin at the question, but the way Creed stared at him forced him not to make a joke of it. Creed knew his question was a bait to a guy such as the one who was cocky enough to stand in front of him eyeballing his girlfriend. You want some is a yes or no question, and it could pertain to him wanting to fight or him wanting to make a couple more moves on Trina. In either case, Creed was preparing him for his loss.

"It's a party right…Creed? I'm just here to have a good time," he finally responded as the music blasted. The confrontation was so quick that Trina missed the entire thing before she stood up on a chair with a long glass filled with juice and whatever it was Grace slipped into the drink. She drank it straight down and in no time was all giggles after also downing one other mini bottle that Grace had shown her from her purse earlier.

Creed turned his back on the guy to continue toward Trina who was gathering the crowd to sing happy birthday to Creed whom she was ecstatic to have in her life again. When he saw her climbing up on the table, he started to laugh. As soon as his laughter ended, the whole crowd started to sing the happy birthday song as Trina did a dance for him atop the table. As Grace stared on, she capped up the bottle of alcohol because she knew that Trina was slowly on her way to getting drunk, and she didn't want to be the only one sober at the party to care for the buzzed crowd. Instead, Grace went and got her private stash of alcohol, took some down and got just right for the night.

Trina continued to dance for Creed as Grace walked up and raised her cup for a toast. The bustling crowd followed, but just as Grace was getting ready to open her mouth and congratulate both Trina and Creed on their wonderful relationship, Trina hopped down from the table and snatched Grace's drink from her hand. The alcohol spilled onto Grace's hair and chest.

"The hell, Trina!" she yelled, but Trina ignored her, continuing to lift the cup high and toast to her man.

"Everybody, I have the best man in the world, so don't any of you broke down females come over here for him," she joked. "And no other woman toasts to this man right here," she stated while placing her arm around his neck, "but me. I love you, Creed," she continued kissing him on his lips. Then, she tossed the drink down her throat, the music turned up, and everyone started dancing once again...except for Grace. She'd already walked away from the toast and the crowd in disbelief at how Trina embarrassed her.

Inside the bathroom, Grace wiped her face and neck off. The alcohol had already run down her shirt causing wet stains in her silk blouse, and while she wiped, she became even angrier. Her blouse was ruined for the night, and she truly didn't want to be at the party any longer.

"She's such an ass when Creed comes around...like he's her knight in shining armor when really his ass just got out of jail from behind damn armor," she grumbled. "Lost her damn mind tossing this drink on me," she continued to complain, believing that Trina did the whole thing to show out on purpose and at her expense. "I'm sick of her doing this shit to me…her perfect acting ass. I got her perfect ass though."

There was a towel hanging up in the bathroom that she used to finish dapping the drink from her face. Her temper wasn't going anywhere fast, so she knew that as soon as she saw Trina again, she would have to pull her aside and let her know to get off her high horse. Grace then placed her hand on the door knob and left the bathroom, dragging her rage along with her.

She spotted Trina dancing with Creed near the top of the open balcony at the top of the stairs while everyone else was downstairs having a good time. Instead of marching up the stairs to snatch her away from Creed, she just went into the entertainment room and got another drink, not feeling like partying at all anymore at all.

About an hour went by until Grace finally saw Trina again. Creed wasn't with her, so she took her opportunity and went after her. Trina was in the kitchen, gathering up what food she could find, and when she saw Grace, she lashed out once again.

"Grace, what the hell? There's no more food, and me and Creed hadn't even eaten yet. Where were you? You let all these people eat all of what we had?"

"Where was I?" Grace asked pointing at her chest. "You got some damn nerve, Trina. First you dump a drink on my face and then you blame me for your damn wack ass party."

"You said you were gonna have my back, Grace, while I talked to Creed, but I didn't have quite the chance to tell him yet. Still working up the nerve to do it." Trina said knowing full well that she'd changed her mind a while ago about having the conversation at all today.

"Forget having your damn back, Trina, because you didn't have mine when you made me look like some damn flunky in front of all these people. Here's the clue, Trina." She walked nose to nose with Trina and continued, "I'm not your sidekick. I got my own life. I just happen to always help you hold your weak ass life together."

Trina didn't say anything back quickly because she was stunned at Grace's words. It hit her to the core of her being and caused all the joy that she had only moments ago to flee. Not willing, at that point, to show that she even cared about what Grace said in the slightest, Trina then retaliated with the only thing she knew would hurt Grace, despite the fact that she didn't purposefully intended to hurt Grace earlier.

"You're just upset that you can't get a man since you got that scar across your face…that none of that damn makeup you put on can hide." Then, she smirked, allowing her bruised ego to rule her words. "Try to go find yourself a man…and stop looking at mine. Hold that shit together."

A tear came down Grace's face, rolling right over the scar that she tried each day to cover up and forget. She'd received her scar from a car accident that she caused but lived to regret every single day. Her face had never looked the same again. Grace could tell that when people first met her, the scar was the first thing they looked at. She could tell by the way their eyes connected with her cheek.

Trina didn't even stick around for Grace to comment, but she knew she'd hit the one nerve Grace was sensitive about. Immediately, as she walked away, she felt sorry about how she left Grace standing there in her own sadness in the middle of her party. She was in the middle of turning back around to apologize to the best friend she loved dearly, however, when she looked back, Grace had already walked away. She was nowhere to be found. When she turned back to look for Creed, he was no longer at the base of the stairs. Therefore, she shook everything off and mingled with the crowd until she inevitably bumped into her again to apologize for what was a misunderstanding.

***

"Creed." When Creed didn't answer, she called again, but this time she walked toward him quickly as he lit a cigarette at the front of the house. "Creed, what's going on?"

"What's up with you, Grace? I had to step out here and get a smoke. Why aren't you in there doing your thing?" he asked blowing the smoke from his nostrils with full knowledge that Grace was one for a good party.

Grace glanced back at the front door and then back at Creed as she stood toe to toe with him. She fiddled with her fingers a bit before saying, "She killed your baby."

Creed blew the smoke from his mouth as he stared back at her, and then he looked away and flicked his cigarette after remaining silent for about ten seconds. He then, rested his back up against the stucco home. As he looked back at Grace who awaited his response, he finally spoke. "What baby are you talking about? I don't have any babies, and who killed my so called baby?"

Even though Creed's demeanor was calm and he spoke in a low tone, Grace could tell that she'd already said enough. Since Trina was going to criticize and make her feel worthless, she would do the job that Trina was too afraid to do, even if it meant their friendship. Besides, after that last stunt, she was tired of being the thread that held all her secrets.

"Trina...she was supposed to tell you tonight, but she didn't. I'm sick of holding things down for her while she figures out the right time to let you know about the abortion."

"So, you're telling me that Trina was pregnant with my baby?" He leaned off the wall and walked closer to Grace, staring her in her eyes.

"That's fucked up, Creed," she said, reaching for his hand. "You have a right to know...and I'm sorry. It was wrong of her not to tell you." He watched her reach and finally attach her hand to his.

"Go get her." He moved his hand from hers, looking at her suspiciously. Then, he repeated himself as he watched her stare back at him like she expected more than the look he was giving her. "Go get her... since you're out here saying shit and touching. Go get her," he stated again, not believing much coming from her mouth.

"Creed, I'm serious. Why the hell you think she broke up with you? Come on," Grace continued, almost like he was causing her excruciating pain by not believing what she knew as the truth.

"What y'all doing over here, I mean, out here, and the party's inside?" Trina asked suspiciously watching Grace as she backed away from Creed. Creed didn't move. Instead, he continued staring at a shaking Grace who nervously turned to Trina.

"Go ahead and have that talk that you needed to have. Did you forget," she hollered out at Trina who stopped in her tracks at Grace's words. "Or do I have to tell him?"

"Grace!" a terrified Trina shouted back, her eyes shifting between her man and her best friend.

Grace then lifted her hands up into the air, mocking the shock that she'd put Trina in. "Trina!" she called back. "Tell him." She then walked toward her, only to bitterly pass by saying, "Since you had so much mouth with me, try having the same amount of mouth with him. I'm outta here. Handle some shit by yourself...for once in your life."

Trina turned back to Creed who still had yet to move from his stance. He stared straight ahead, obviously awaiting her response to Grace's accusation. Suddenly, the music that she heard from inside the house faded, leaving her to face her deepest secret yet. Tears began to roll down her face as she approached

Creed, and she quickly wiped them in an attempt to maintain some sense of control over herself and the situation.

The grass beneath her feet reminded her of thorns with each step she took toward the man she loved. There was never a time that she felt so discouraged in his presence, and there was never a time that she didn't know what to say or do. She stood in front of him, nearly in the same exact spot where Grace once stood, but Creed looked right over her head. That was how she knew that Grace had already told him…that and the tears she spotted growing in his eyes.

"Creed," she stumbled, but he didn't answer. Instead, his eyes wandered slowly down her long V-neck blouse and remained stagnant at her navel. "I didn't tell you because I didn't know what to do myself and you were locked up, then we broke up…"

Creed reached over and rubbed her cheek. He then walked closer to her and placed his hand over her stomach. "You took my baby from me, Trina?" When she looked into his eyes with no response, Creed simply walked around her, leaving her in the grass while he walked back to his car. He never turned around once, and she never turned back to follow him. She continued to stare at the stucco home, and suddenly, the sound of the music came back to her ears, forcing her to remove the tears and get herself back together. Without even looking up as she passed by each person, she walked inside her party and ended everything with one loud…

"Party over."

As she stood there atop the balcony, her guests did nothing but stare back at her at first. Then, when Trina looked at the button pushing DJ, he knew she was serious and wanted him to take the pre-recorded music and get out. He didn't waste any time.

"Take as much food and drinks with you as you like," Trina continued because she already had too much to clean up by herself. The fact of the matter was that all she wanted to do was go to sleep. She couldn't call Creed no matter what because of her parents logging her line, meaning that there was no real way to contact him but through Grace who was gone.

As the crowd cleared out, Trina got the floor vacuum and started to suck up anything remaining on the hardwoods. During the vacuuming, she slowly went from sad to enraged at the thought of Grace revealing her secret to Creed, so much so that she started to tear up again.

"You alright, Trina?" a girl stopped before leaving to check on her after noticing her tears. "I can help with this mess if you..."

"No just go. My party, my mess. Thanks." Trina just kept vacuuming until everyone exited, mainly so she wouldn't have to look up at anyone else. As soon as the last person left, she locked the doors, sat down on the floor, and erupted into tears as the vacuum continued to hum over her weeping.

The water hit her skin from the back like a tidal wave as she stood in the shower, still in tears over what was supposed to be a great night. She peeked over at her cell phone hoping that Creed would call from someone else's number to talk to her, and she was even tempted to call his phone as well. The way things were with her mom and dad, they would end up on the next flight back if they even saw a trace of Creed's number on the list alerting them to the fact that he was out of jail. There were no flashes of light coming from her smartphone, so she simply sat down in the shower, not even caring that the water was beating down on her freshly done ponytail. Her night couldn't have gotten any worse.

Laying her head sideways atop her knees, the water pounded her face. Finally, she leaned over and turned the water completely off. The sound of the water leaving through the drain exacerbated what just happened in her life as she drew a comparison between it and the meltdown that just happened hours ago at her home. In the middle of her thoughts, she got out of the shower, grabbed her towel and wrapped it around herself while dialing Grace's number. As the phone rang on the other end, she grew furious, so when the answering machine picked up, she slammed the phone onto the plush rug beneath her feet. After sitting at the edge of the tub angrily kicking the wall, she stood up with another idea.

She exited the bathroom and ran into her room to toss on another pair of shorts and a tank top. From there, she took off her fake and now wet and mangled ponytail that she wore for the party, and let her real hair down. After combing it out, blow drying and giving it another quick do with the flat iron, she walked down the hallway into her parents' bedroom.

"I know they still have that house phone tucked around here somewhere. Do they even pay for the line still though?" she asked herself as she placed her hand on the doorknob, about to unlock it with the key. However, with the slightest turn, the door came open. Trina paused before going inside. "I thought I locked this door," she whispered to herself a bit confused at how the door was open. She recalled twisting each of the bedroom doorknobs upstairs to make sure they were locked tight before the party even got started.

Quickly, Trina turned around and walked to the other rooms, besides hers, to check if they were locked, and they were. While she was checking, she decided to go ahead and unlock them all, chucking her parents' unlocked bedroom door up to a mere accident. There were four bedrooms upstairs, therefore, she walked inside each room and cracked the windows so that any odor from the party would seep out before her parents got back.

"I'll leave all these doors open just in case the funk traveled upstairs," she stated as she walked back to her parents' room, but before she entered, she heard what sounded like a knock from downstairs. "The heck was that?" Then, she thought about it. "I know people aren't still coming for the party." She shook her head and went back into her bedroom. Inside her drawer was a piece of paper and pen, and with it, she wrote in big letters *Go home. Party over.* She then, snatched a piece of tape, stuck it on the paper and headed downstairs.

"It figures people would still be coming over here after midnight," she complained. "Sorry guys. Closed down," she sang with a fully blossomed note of irritation. As soon as she got downstairs, she approached the front door and then hesitated. "Creed?" she asked herself hoping that the knock she heard was actually him, so instead of continuing on her steady walk to the arched doors, she ran, only taking about five leaps to reach the knob. Without even asking who was on the other side, her desperation caused her to swing the door open.

"Creed?" she asked when she saw no one there. Only the scenery of an abandoned street stared back at her, and Trina's heart sunk. She then took the paper sign and slammed it against the front door. Looking around once again to see if she saw anyone, she finally shut the front door, locked it, and went into the entertainment room.

"They might have one tucked down here somewhere," she stated referring to a landline phone. Beneath the widescreen television was a solid oak entertainment stand with cabinets. She rushed over to it, but the cabinets where locked. "Who does that?" she yelled completely frustrated. Seconds later, her cell phone rang from upstairs. "Dang it!"

Trina took off up the stairs and into her bedroom where she thought the ring was coming from. When she didn't see it on the bed or dresser, she lunged into the bathroom which was the only other place she thought it would be. Then, the ringing stopped. She spun around in the bathroom, but there was no sign of her cell phone.

"Where's my damn phone?" she groaned while stomping her feet in disgust, feeling like she was missing a call from her one and only Creed. "I just had it… like just now!" She stormed out of the bathroom on the way back to her room when the cell phone rang again. Trina turned back to look down the hall because she couldn't understand why the chime of her cell phone was coming from further down the hall…in her parents' room.

"I didn't even...the world?" She quickly paced to the master bedroom and pushed the door open to find her cell phone in the middle of the neatly made king sized bed. In shock, she turned to look behind herself, only to retrace where she thought she'd gone. Not once did she remember fully entering the master bedroom to put her cell down. Slightly cautious, she pushed the room door all the way back until it hit the wall. The cell phone stopped ringing, but paranoia overcame Trina causing her not to move another inch.

Everything in the room was just as her mother would leave it. Trina counted the same five pillows that decorated the five hundred ply sheets that layered the bed. Each picture frame stood perfectly from smallest to tallest on the dresser while the master bathroom door remained open, just as her mother liked it when the bedroom was empty. The cell phone began to ring again.

Slowly, she walked into the room, her anxiety increasing with every step. Then, in a split second, she dashed to the bed, leaped atop it, grabbed the phone, and then slammed her back against the headboard.

"Hello? Hello?" she repeated, not even looking at the caller ID. When no one answered, she pushed the phone closer to her ear, but when she heard nothing, she pulled the phone back to see the cell phone's screen. As soon as she pulled the phone away from her face, the screen lit up. There were words written on the wallpaper addressed to Trina that stated "This is not your phone."

"Shit!" Trina threw the phone across the room and screamed in terror before she accidentally shoved herself backwards off the elevated bed. Only seconds after falling onto the floor, she began to scramble, looking for the landline. "Come on, come on," she whimpered as she yanked the dresser drawers out, and when she couldn't find the phone there, she fell flat on her stomach to see if it was underneath the bed. Before she was able to crawl from underneath, the cell phone that mimicked hers down to the ringer, began to sound off again.

Tears began to fall down her eyes as she moved from underneath the bed to stare at it. Her eyes, then, floated to the open bedroom door. "Whoever the hell is still in here better stop playing these damn games and get out! Beating your ass is the last thing I want to do today for going inside my phone and changing all my shit around," she yelled, slapping the floor with her hand as her fear began to turn into anger after figuring someone was playing a mean joke. "Now, leave. The party has been over! Get the hell out of my house," she continued as she stood up, took a deep breath and then marched toward what she believed was her pranked cell phone.

As soon as she got to it, she snatched it from the floor, and it stopped ringing once again. She checked the text messages to prove to herself that it was really her phone, but when she looked, there were none. Then she went directly to the phone book where all of the contacts she thought she had were all gone. Suddenly, a text message came through. She opened it, and it read…"I told you this isn't your phone…but this is your house…and I'm in it."

Trina's mouth began to tremble as she stared at not only the message, but the number that registered with the text. It was hers. The phone dropped from her hand like a heavy weight and pounded the floor. Her hands shook uncontrollably, and even though her mouth was wide open, not a sound came out. She stood there paralyzed in fear while her eyes moved quickly back and forth around her as though she didn't already see that the room was empty. Another message came in through the phone as the tears floated down her eyes at the same time she peered at the bedroom door, causing her to shudder.

"I'm not reading it! Get out of my house!" she screamed through her weeping. As she screamed, the cell phone continued to vibrate and ring which signified more messages. When she looked down, with each five seconds, there was a new message. "Get out! Leave me alone," she screamed until she saw a shoebox at the side of her mom's bed. She dove for it because she knew it housed at least a six inch heel because her mom wasn't the sneaker kind of woman. "I'm gonna beat your ugly ass if I so much as see you…" As she spoke, she was interrupted by the sound of footsteps rushing up the staircase. Shaken by the sound, she rushed to the side of the bedroom door, escaping her fear for the seconds that she decided to fight back.

Trina held the heel up high with her body plastered against the wall in hopes that whoever was coming up the stairs would take a pounding from the heel that was in her hand. Her breathing was beyond rapid, and just as she got ready to swing, there were no more footsteps. She pushed her head against the wall, but there was still nothing more to hear, like whoever it was went down the stairs but not up.

"Jesus, please, help me," she whispered as she gathered the courage to quickly glance into what became the longest hallway that she'd ever seen. There was no one there. She looked back at the cell phone. Instead of going on her first impulse which was to run, she dashed back to the phone. When she picked it up, she opened the messages that were on the home phone screen. It warned, "Call the police, and I'll kill you before they get here."

Trina quickly looked up at the room door and then back at the phone as she cried silently, trying her best not to make more noise than what she already had. Suddenly, instead of dialing the cops, she began dialing another number – Creed's. As the phone rang, she backed up in horror from the bedroom door, moving backward toward the bathroom, but when she got Creed's voice mail instead of his voice, she panicked and ended the call. The next person she called was her father as she hid behind the wall of the bathroom.

"Pick up, daddy, just pick up," she begged as she slid down the bathroom wall, and the answering machine picked up. "Daddy, come back home. Don't call the cops because he's gonna kill me if you call the cops," she rambled. "I need you to come home because someone is in the house with me, and he's gonna kill me. He has my phone."

Another message came through to the phone from her cell phone, but she ignored it as she ran to her dad's nightstand, remembering that he used to keep a knife taped to the bottom of the drawer. She yanked the whole drawer from the stand, and there it was, taped to the drawer's backside. She snatched it off frantically and dialed Creed again as the silent echo of the house remained in her ears, standing alert for any sound that would put her in a position where she had to use the blade. Again, she got Creed's answering machine.

"Creed, this isn't a joke. I need your help back at my house. Either someone broke in while I was in the shower, or somebody didn't leave the party and now they are trying to kill me. Don't call the cops because I'll be dead before they get here. Just come back and get me, please…I got nobody else!" she explained at a whisper's tone, choking back tears. She, then, shoved the telephone in her pocket.

Her hands trembled as she moved toward the bedroom door. "Forget this shit. I'm gonna get the hell up outta here," she started in a quiet tone in an attempt to boost her confidence." At that point, she raised the knife, and with each step, took a deep breath, focusing all her attention on getting out of the house alive. "Oh Jesus, please, help me," she continued, as she took one last breath before peeking around the corner and down the hallway. It was just how she left it – empty. She then placed herself back into her parents' bedroom, pushed the cell phone deeper into her pocket, gripped the knife even tighter, and bolted from the room. Trina was headed to the front door.

With the knife in her right hand and her feet moving as fast as they could, she didn't look to her right or to her left. The only place she wanted to be was through the front door, but when she got to the edge of the stairs, she spun around to check the hallway behind her. Her chest pounded and as she held on to the knife, ready to stab anyone who showed up. When she saw no one, she immediately ran down the stairs, and as soon as she placed her bare feet on the hardwoods, her heart felt glad because she was only paces from the door. However, when she turned to run towards it, it was wide open, with the note she left on it flapping in the light breeze.

"The fuck!" she cried. "Why is my door open?" she screamed, her confidence caved while she pondered the fact that she might be getting set up to die. "Why is my freakin' front door open, you crazy *ass*?" she yelled, spinning around, paranoid at all the open space around her. She wished her back was against a wall, however, she was vulnerable on every side. The cell phone rang again, and she quickly grabbed it from her pocket, however, when she read that the call was coming from her cell phone, she got frustrated and threw it against the wall. The phone shattered into pieces, and she hollered, "Fuck you!"

At that point, she thought about nothing else but getting through the front door, therefore, she started run her hardest. As her feet hit the floor, all she could see was her life before her as she imagined herself running as far away from her home as she could. There weren't any neighbors close by, but it didn't matter to her. All that mattered was that she got out from where the danger was, and that was located where she was exiting. Her feet hit the doorway, and suddenly out of nowhere, there was Grace directly in front of her...being held up and restrained by a man wearing a mask, her mouth taped and her eyes bulging out of the sockets in fear, as the knife Trina was holding plunged directly into her stomach. Grace, with her arms reaching toward Trina for help, moaned in pain. However, instead of pulling her, Trina screamed in horror.

"Grace!" Trina fell backwards onto the floor and scrambled toward Grace as the masked man allowed her best friend to fall to the floor atop the knife. "No! Grace!" a frantic Trina hollered while the unknown man stepped inside the house and slowly shut the door while staring at a helpless Trina roll her lifeless friend over onto her back. "Grace," she continued to call and shake her until she felt the intruder getting closer.

"Get the fuck away from me!" she screamed from the floor, enraged at the intruder that somehow knew her, but she had no idea who he was. He wore all black. There was nothing that she could gather from how he truly appeared behind all the clothing he wore. Despite the warm night, the assailant also wore a black sweatshirt that zipped down in the front, but as he walked toward Trina, he started to zip it back up.

Quickly, she finally scrambled to her feet and ran toward the back door, screaming for her life as she felt the presence of a delusional man behind her as he called her name.

"Trina," he sang, his voice deep and raspy. "Trina, I love you, Trina. I can't live without you, Trina."

Trina's entire body slammed against the back door, and as she tried to open it, for some reason she couldn't fathom, it wouldn't open. "Come on!" she yelled frantically as the man she was trying to escape got closer. His voice grew louder and louder, and when she couldn't take it anymore, she spun around ready to fight for her life. "Stop singing my name. Just leave me alone!"

Once she turned to face and fight her attacker, she stared down the spacious corridor as if she was staring down the barrel of a gun, but she saw no one. Paralyzed by the unknown, her eyes shifted back and forth for any signs of movement as her best friend lay there at the front door dead. Trina buckled under the pressures that seemed to be crushing her life away, and as she fell to the floor in tears and begging for her life, confused at why she couldn't get out of her own house, she spotted her phone in the middle of the floor.

"No, no, no," she cried repeatedly as she turned around facing the door once again, trying to force the thought of running to her phone away from her mind because she knew it was another trap. Once again she grabbed the backdoor's knob but it failed to unlock no matter how many time she turned it. "Open!" she screamed at the top of her lungs, but the door was somehow jammed, unwilling to open no matter how hard she pulled.

At the back of the house was the laundry area that she rushed into and began to wildly look for anything she could find to use for a weapon. Feeling like she could hyperventilate, she leaned over on a shelf and took some deep breaths, nearly ready to give up until she saw the washing powder. She shoved the other items from the shelf causing them to hit the floor all at once just so she could grab a hand full of detergent in her right hand. She wasted no time. She ran out of the laundry room straight toward the staircase as she ignored the cell phone that started to ring…until she glanced down quickly at it to notice that it was Creed. For only a moment she stalled, but she knew that Creed couldn't help her, so instead of reaching for the telephone, she bolted to a staircase that led not to the upstairs bedrooms, but to the apartment in the basement. In order to even get inside the place, there was a code in, and no one was supposed to know the code except her and her parents.

Gripping the laundry detergent in one hand, just in case she needed it to blind the man who was coming for her life, she bolted down the small flight of stairs and like lightening punched in the code. It worked, and as soon as she went inside, she locked the door. Then, she bolted to the other door that led to the outside to lock it as well. She did all that with the lights completely off, and not once did she think to turn one light on which left her in total darkness. Only her mental notes of how her father had things set up in the basement kept her at ease. It was a place hardly anyone came, especially guests much less strangers, therefore, there was no way anyone would know how to locate her without lights. She made her way to the corner of a wall that could see both doors, and she stalled there, listening to her cell phone constantly ring right above her head through the ceiling.

***

"Pick up the phone, Trina, damn girl," Creed complained as he drove as fast as he could back to Trina's house. He'd only gotten Trina's message minutes ago as he stepped out of the shower from taking in the worst news that he could possibly have gotten on his twentieth birthday of his baby being aborted. Despite it all, he'd always promised Trina that he would love her, and that wasn't going to change, baby or not, together or not. The fact was that when he heard her message on the phone, there wasn't any other place he was going to be, and that was to beat the person down at her house trying to take her life.

As he drove, he continued to press redial on his phone, going back and forth between the number Trina called him on and her real cell phone number. Neither one of them were being picked up, therefore, he grabbed at his glove compartment handle. When he opened it, he felt around quickly in efforts to try and keep himself on the road.

"Man, damn!" he slammed the glove compartment shut, upset that he'd left his pistol. Being that he'd just got out of jail, he asked his dad to lift everything from his car, and in doing so, the pistol went with him. He hadn't even checked to see if his father placed it back at his bed post. Fortunately for the time at hand, Creed had a pair of brass knuckles with him that his own father didn't know about which were taped to the bottom of his seat. "Gonna have to work with these." Creed reached underneath his seat and ripped them from the bottom.

"Hello, you've reached Trina..."

Creed pressed the end button on his cell phone and stopped calling altogether as he rounded the corner to her street. He saw no signs of an intrusion as he sped into the driveway of the house, however, that made no difference to him. The sound of Trina's voice on the phone made him know beyond a shadow of a doubt that she was telling the complete truth. Armed with his brass knuckles, he rushed up to the front door, knocked and dialed her number again at the same time. From the outside of the door, he heard Trina's phone ringing to the call of his.

***

Trina glanced up at the ceiling from her crouched position on the floor of the basement apartment where she was hiding out. Not only did she hear the ringing of her cell phone, but she heard the doorbell ringing as well as constant banging. She then stood up from the floor and ran over to the direction of the front door of the house. That was where she heard the voice of Creed.

"Creed," she said softly as her adrenaline rushed without her having the slightest idea of how to get his attention without him getting killed in the process. The last thing she wanted to do was scream out for him, but what other choice did she have? He could easily think that she's already dead. Therefore, she screamed out his name.

"Creed! Creed, I'm down here in the basement! Creed, I'm okay. He's still here! Don't try to go inside! Creed," she continued to yell at the top of her lungs, and when she heard her phone stop ringing, she felt Creed may have heard her screaming. He knew how to get to the basement door that led outside to the backyard, so she ran to the door to wait, despite the fact that she had no idea if he was on the way or not.

On the way to the door, she heard the code being punched from the other door. She stalled and watched, completely surrounded by the darkness, yet confident that the assailant couldn't get inside. After the four buttons were punched, nothing happened. Trina held her breath, but still, the door wasn't opening. Therefore, she turned back around, still completely locked inside, afraid to run out and miss Creed if he was coming from another direction.

Suddenly, she heard a sound at the other door that made her turn around and stare through the darkness. Completely quiet, she listened for the sound of the door coming open. She didn't hear it. Instead, she heard the sound of the door shutting. He'd gotten inside.

"Oh God," she cried as she turned to unlock the door. As soon as it opened, she bolted out and collided with Creed which knocked her to the ground. Quickly, she scrambled up screaming in terror as Creed forced her up faster by pulling her arm.

"Let's go," he stated as they both took off across the huge backyard. Trina continued to look back as she ran, and Creed simply forced her forward with his faster pace as she held on tightly with both hands.

"Is he close?"

"No...no, he's not even coming," she panted, but then slammed into his body as she turned back around.

"What the hell is this, T?" he asked, catching her before she fell. There was a long rope tied to the back door, and it traveled all the way to the empty pool that was in the process of being fixed. The rope had so much tension in it that it looked like it was set up for some sort of attack, but they both questioned what was on the other end of the rope causing it to pull so tightly.

"I don't know...let's just go," she begged him, looking all around but no sign of the intruder in sight. Creed crossed over the rope and lifted Trina over it, making sure she didn't touch it for fear of a deadly surprise. However, immediately after lifting Trina, he saw a portion of a human body at the floor of the empty pool.

Creed's hand flew atop his head as he allowed the visual of the dead body to sink in as he followed the rope to its end...tied around the person's neck. He didn't say anything, but he didn't have to because the look on his face said it all. Trina let go of him and leaned over to get a glimpse into the pool, and when she finally saw what had Creed so shook up, her fears deepened as she belted out a horrible scream. Creed pulled her away.

"Jeremy!" she screamed. "No, no, he wasn't supposed to be here until tomorrow night, Creed. He killed him," she cried helplessly as she pieced together the complete puzzle of her inability to open the back door. It was because the weight of Jeremy's dead body on the rope forced the door to remain shut.

"Listen, let's go!" Creed yelled, but Trina pointed at the house hysterically.

"He killed Grace, Creed. She's in there. He made me do it. I didn't even see her coming."

"What the hell you talkin' about?"

"I was running, and he pushed her in front of me and the knife...it went inside her," she cried. "But, Creed, she might still be alive. I didn't check, and we have to get her…" she continued, attempting to move him toward the house.

"Look, Trina. We're not going back in the damn house. We're safer outside. Now, I'm gonna have to toss you over this stone wall. You ready?"

"Creed, no! He might be over there," she stated, twisting around to look all over the yard which was pitch black.

"I can't get you over the wall any other way, Trina, unless you have the key to the gate your father keeps locked tight. You don't even have enough strength to jump that thing," he continued quickly. "Look, I'll put you over, and I'll be right behind you. It's a run and jump for me. That's all. Turn around. See?" he said pointing out all over the yard. "You said it yourself. He's not here. He went back inside because he didn't follow us out. He probably saw me and is thinking up another game plan. You got no choice, T," he said out of breath and frustrated. "Now, let's go. I'll be over to meet you in five seconds flat."

Trina stared back at him, but she knew he was right. Swiftly, she said, "Okay, okay, get me up." From there, Trina climbed on top of Creed's back, and he stood back up with her right up against the edge of the stone wall.

"All clear?"

"Yeah, yeah, let me climb over. Hurry up behind me, Creed, please," Trina begged as she boosted herself up with her arms and then dropped to the other side. As soon as she planted her feet on the other side, she turned around to watch her own back while she heard Creed give the word.

"I'm on my way," Creed assured her as he ran back to gather the speed he needed to hop the stone wall. When he started to run forward, he pushed it as hard as he could and jumped onto the wall, getting to the top on the first try. However, when he jumped over, Trina wasn't there. "Trina," he called in a low whisper, believing she was hiding somewhere. He turned around a full three hundred sixty degrees, but no matter where his eyes traveled in the darkness, he couldn't find her. He began to get anxious and paced forward nervously. "Trina, come on…where are you?"

"Creed, Creed, I'm over here," Trina finally responded hiding behind a huge tree at the side of the yard.

"Trina," Creed stated, relieved as he ran over to her, ready to get her to safety. "Did you get a good look at the dude for a description before we go to the cops?" he asked as he grabbed Trina's hand while they headed for his car at the front of the yard.

"No! No wait!"

"What?" Creed asked frustrated as he stopped in his tracks.

"Why are we going to the front of the house? We're out. Let's just run."

"I'm going to get my car, and you're coming, too." He looked behind her at the long winding road that leads away from her home. "There's no way that we can get down that road fast enough. We don't even know who this dude is. Let's go."

"No!" She snatched her hand back from him. "Like hell I'm going back over there! He's there, Creed. I can feel it, and he's waiting."

"Look, you coming?"

"Creed," she pleaded with him, hoping that he wouldn't leave her to get his car. "Please, I'm begging you not to go back over there. Did you see what he did to Jeremy…and how about Grace? You didn't see what happened so you don't know. He's evil, and he will try to kill you, too."

He stared back at her in disbelief. "The same way you killed my baby? There isn't too much difference, is there? So I should fuckin' fear his ass and not fear you?"

"Creed, that's not fair!" she cried.

50

"What is fair, Trina? I still love you, so at least don't let me lose you, too, without giving me a say. You gotta come on."

Trina hopelessly stared back at Creed and then back at the house where two of her friends lay dead. Then, she finally made her decision. She gave her hand back to Creed.

"Now let's go. We'll get in the car, and then we'll have nothing to worry about." They both begin hustling toward the front yard as he dwelled on the life that was already taken from him. "I won't let anything happen to you, T. I wouldn't have let anything happen to my baby either. Fuck being scared and shit. Just do what you have to do...just like we're doing now."

"Creed, I'm sorry...let's just go, alright?" she replied, checking every inch around her as they headed cautiously to the car.

Creed didn't say anything else. Instead, he watched ahead of himself, ready to attack anything that came his way, but what he didn't count on was threat that was about to come barreling toward him.

"Wait, wait," he stated, stopping in his tracks. "My car is moved. He remembered the angle at which he drove into Trina's yard, and instead of being at that same angle, the car was facing them. The lights weren't on, and the car wasn't even running, but it was turned facing them.

Trina grabbed at his shirt. "What do you mean your car is moved? Don't you have your keys, babe?"

There was a dead silence. Creed placed his hand at her mouth for her to keep quiet, and then he pointed to the side of the house, a silent way of telling her that they need to go back with Trina's original plan of running.

"Babe, don't you have..."

As she spoke, the car lights came on high beam, and then the car's engine started up. She quickly glanced up at Creed, stunned that he left the keys in the ignition. Creed motioned her to start running, and as he motioned to her, he heard the car start to move quickly toward him.

"Trina, go!"

"Creed, come on!" she screamed as she backed away frantically.

"Move!" Creed yelled as he watched her run away as fast as she could. The car came barreling towards him, and Creed stood his ground, ready to pounce on the intruder who tried to take the life of the girl he loved. He moved to the side, hoping to shatter the driver's side window, but just then, the car made a slight turn away from Creed. It was headed toward Trina.

"Trina!"

Trina stopped in her tracks and turned back around, unsure of what was happening behind her. She then saw Creed running her way…behind the car that was headed directly for her. There was nowhere to hide in the well sculpted yard.

"Creed!" Suddenly, she started running again, but this time, she ran in a crooked line, trying her best to shake the driver. No matter how hard she tried, he kept coming, despite her efforts to have him wreck the car into the big oak tree. All the driver did was weave around the tree, pressing harder on the gas, just to try and kill her.

Trina's efforts to get away were being halted by her body running out of breath. She didn't know how much more she could run, and as she looked back the car was right there behind her. He was toying with her. Every time she took a step, he pressed on the gas only enough to tap the back of her leg, causing her to fall.

She cried, "Creed, please, help me! He's crazy!" Trina toppled to the ground as the car continued to hit her from behind each time she tried to get up.

"Trina!" Creed called as he ran up to the back of the car, and in seconds, the car went in reverse, hitting Creed in the knee. He fell over in excruciating pain. That didn't stop him from getting to Trina, however, and by the time the two locked hands, the driver had gone, leaving them watching the car from behind.

Creed continued trying to move, but cried out in agony each time he moved his leg. Trina, feeling pressed to do something fast, stood up to try and lift him onto his feet. "Come on, Creed, pull yourself up."

"I got it. I got it," he struggled but finally made it up.

"We have to get back to the house. He's not there, so let's get back, and call the cops."

"Yeah, let's do that," Creed answered. "I could kill that mother…"

"Don't worry about him. He's gone, right now. There's no way you need to be on this leg. We'll get back in and lock up. Cops will be here soon."

"And your folks, right?"

Trina didn't answer him. The last thing she was going to think about was her parents and what they thought. The fact was that her friends were dead in her house while it was Creed who tried to save her life on the day he got out of jail, and for that matter, on his birthday. He almost died himself.

"Give me those," she said referring to his brass knuckles.

"No, let me keep them just…"

"Give them to me. If we are going to call the cops, the last thing they need to see you with are these. Let me put them somewhere, under my mattress."

"I'll give them to you when we get inside."

"Why not now?" Trina asked tired and frustrated with everything, including Creed's resistance to her word. He'd already almost gotten both of them killed by not listening to her in the first place when she asked him to not go back toward the house, and now he wouldn't give her the brass knuckles.

"Why do you think he didn't kill us? He was the one with my car, Trina. He injured me, and he taunted you like it was some joke. Why do you think?"

She turned to look behind them, and there the car was. It was sitting in the darkness with the lights off. Trina then turned back to Creed.

"He's back there, Creed," her voice trembled as she gathered the energy and strength to help him even more as they approached the porch steps. "Don't look back. Let's just climb these steps and get in."

Creed looked back anyway, and as soon as he did, the lights of his car came on, and the car began to roll forward. Trina heard the roar of the car, and she began to pull Creed by the arm as he hopped up the steps. When she looked up, the car was headed straight for them at top speed.

"Creed, come on! He's gunning it! We have to get inside!"

"Go open the door!"

Trina ran to the door and turned, but it was locked. "Shit!" The keypad was the other option she had to opening the door, and her fingers shook with each number she pressed. The light turned green and the door unlocked. She turned to face Creed who was almost to the top step when the car rammed into the bottom steps.

"He knows the code! Come on, Creed. He knows. He has to know the code."

"You fuckin' serious?"

"I don't know, but he probably does," she responded, recalling his entry into the basement. "Hurry! Grab my hand."

Creed reached up and lunged forward, falling onto the top of the porch within arm's reach of the front door. Trina began to pull him as hard as she could when the door of the car opened, and the intruder stepped out slowly, looking directly at Trina.

"Creed, you have to push!" she yelled, watching her attacker begin walking up the steps just as Creed's foot cleared the front door.

"I'm in, I'm in! Lock the door, T."

Trina shoved the door closed and locked it as Creed pushed himself up against it while he stared at a dead Grace laying directly in front of him on the floor.

"Go get something to jam the door up, just in case he can get it with the code. Hurry up."

"I'm trying, Creed, but I don't know what… I can't find anything!" she screamed back, searching for anything that could block the door. She came up with nothing. Running back to the door, she stood next to Creed who was already on his feet, watching the assailant come closer to the door. He gripped his brass knuckles and then looked at Trina.

"You got something though, right …in case these knuckles don't do the trick?" he asked as he leaned up against the wall.

Trina had already grabbed a knife from the kitchen. "I'm not fuckin' stupid."

"And this ain't no fuckin' movie. People die for real, so you better be ready to kill him in case you're the last one standing."

"Creed, don't say stuff like that. We're both gonna make it," she said preparing herself to fight along with Creed.

He turned to look at her. "I promised you a long time ago, nobody's gonna hurt you as long as I'm alive to stop 'em."

As he spoke, there was a large bang at the door that shook it like it was being hit with more than just a kick or a punch.

"What the hell is that?" Trina shuddered.

"Brace yourself. As a matter of fact, go run to the kitchen and get another knife. Do it fast. I can't see him."

Trina ran off and retrieved another knife from the drawer, and then she stopped on the way up, turned back around and got a hammer from underneath the sink. By the time she got back to the door, there was a huge crack in the center of the arched doors. As she passed by Grace on the floor, her knees buckled once again, but Creed got her attention.

"Stop looking at her, and if you do, think of that as yourself. Then, use Grace's memory to beat his ass."

They both stood there at the door, ready to kill. Creed leaned up against the wall with the hammer in his hand and Trina standing directly in front of the door to take the first stab when Creed caused him to hit the floor. There was another bang at the door, and Creed lunged forward believing that the man was coming through, however, he didn't. As they waited for another hit at the door, things went quiet. They both looked at each other while confusion took over their faces.

Creed finally put his head to the sliding peephole, glanced over at Trina, and quickly slid the cover back to peer out. With a quick glance that lasted only one second, he slid the cover back over the peephole, and then shook his head at Trina, signifying that the man was nowhere in sight.

"Are the other doors locked?"

Trina's face turned ghastly as she stared back into Creed's eyes. Then, she turned in the direction of the back door where the rope tied to Jeremy kept it from opening from the inside, but not the outside. Trina bolted to the back door as Creed moved to a loveseat that sat in the room to the right. With all the strength that was in him, he shoved the loveseat over in front of the door, if for nothing but to give them extra time to work out a plan to kill him or get away.

He reached for his cell phone as Trina came running back towards him. "Give me my phone, T."

"Your phone?"

"Yeah, my phone? What…you don't have it?"

"No, Creed, I don't," she whined. "I don't have mine either," she answered, searching the floor for the phone she left earlier when Creed was calling. "He must have it. I left it here, right here."

"That means unless you still have landlines lit up around here, we have to come up with another plan. My phone's not on me, babe."

"Wait. My computer."

"Where is it?"

"It's upstairs in the room," she answered, but then she thought about something better. "My dad. He has a computer downstairs. It stays off, but I know his password. I can get inside. It's easier for you to go downstairs, right?"

"Yeah, yeah. Let's go."

They both rushed down the staircase that led to the basement apartment, and when Trina pressed the code, she rushed inside, headed directly to the computer. She pressed the power on the laptop, and began tapping the desk with her fingers. "Hurry up!"

Creed limped inside, able to handle the pain in his knee a little bit better since the shock of the hit. As he crossed the floor toward Trina, he caught movement to his right, and he immediately glanced up to the outline of a man standing outside of the open door.

"Trina, go upstairs. Go upstairs now."

"What?" Trina asked, unsure of what was going on as she started to type her dad's password.

"Trina, listen to me," he stated again as he watched their attacker step inside. His eyes weren't even on Creed. Instead, the unidentified man kept his eyes on Trina. "You need to go back upstairs."

Trina then looked up, and then noticed Creed staring at the door. "Oh God…" she choked as she became aware of what was happening. "I forgot about this door. It was left unlocked, Creed," she cried, moving over near him.

"I love you, Trina. Tell him about us, baby, will you? You are gonna tell him, aren't you?" the man sang.

"Trina you know this dude from somewhere?"

"No!" Trina screeched.

Then the man stopped suddenly. He tilted his head, and then, stared squarely at Trina as if she said the wrong thing. At that point, he removed his ski mask, and there he was.

Trina's stomach got weak as she remembered that she had seen and even spoken to her attacker before. It was in the grocery store, earlier when she and Grace were picking up the food.

~~

"Hey, I'm going to grab some extra goodies for the party while you wait here. I'm not in the mood to stand around and do nothing, so I'll be right back," Grace stated as she moseyed off further into the grocery store. Meanwhile, Trina stood there thumbing through a catalog that showcased the variety of cakes and other desserts the grocery store had to offer…until a young man came and interrupted her.

He was a tall, light brown and extremely handsome African American male. His eyes were light brown, and it was his smile that caught the attention of Trina as he spoke to her for the first time.

"Is it your birthday?"

"No, no…it's not my birthday. Just thumbing through while I wait on a cake."

"So there is a party somewhere in town? I plan on ordering a cake as well. Name's Evan. Nice to meet you."

"Trina," she blushed as she continued to look him over quickly. "Not bad…" she continued and then clarified herself, "the selection I mean."

"Do you mind if I share this space with you to look things over. I still haven't chosen exactly what I want yet. What do you think I should get for a festive occasion for my sister who's seventeen."

"Oh, well, this one is cute," she stated pointing at the cake photo. "I got this one for the party I'm throwing tonight. It's wonderful, and I love chocolate. If that's her flavor, then…" she paused suddenly because from the side of her eye, she noticed he wasn't staring at the book. Instead, he was staring all over her, from her hair to her waist and even her legs which made her uneasy. "Yeah, here, feel free." She quickly handed him the whole catalog and backed away. He continued to stare at her for about two more seconds, not even paying attention to the fact that she'd just placed the book into his hand. Finally, he spoke again, almost dazed.

"Thank you…for your help, Trina."

59

"Yeah…uh…bye." Quickly, Trina turned away from the man, who in her eyes went from cute to creepy, until Grace came back and startled her with the news of Creed being out of lock up. As Grace was in mid sentence, a quick glance relieved Trina as the man she knew as Evan was gone. Trina thought no more of it.

~~

"This was supposed to be our party, baby," he stated as he walked closer. "We even picked out a cake together, and you told me to come back to the house to meet you here."

Trina began to cry while Creed grabbed her arm. "Trina, who is this?"

"He told me his name was Evan. I don't know this guy," she whimpered. "When I was waiting for the other cake to finish at the grocery store today, he came up and looked at the catalog with me. That's it. He told me his name, and I told him mine. It was right before I saw you…like minutes before."

"How did he know where you live?" Creed asked as he backed her behind him.

"I don't know, Creed! I don't know!"

"Grace, told me," the intruder interrupted, behaving slightly annoyed. "She told me when you left out of the store," he stated, flipping his demeanor back to a happy one. "I told her that you invited me, and even she was happy. The more the merrier, she said. See, even Grace was happy to see me until…she got in your way."

"You fuckin' liar! You killed her. You pushed her onto my knife at the door. You tricked her, you fuckin' psycho!" Trina screamed, but Creed, feeling the situation get out of control, pushed her back, and approached him calmly yet cautiously.

The intruder watched Creed carefully as he walked toward him. He looked slightly amused at Creed, how he seemed to walk steady on his limp. Slowly, as Creed got closer, he lifted the hammer that he got from Trina and began to speak.

"Looks like we got ourselves a misunderstanding. See, this is *my* girl, and this party turned into one for me on *my* birthday. Do you understand that? Now, maybe you have a damn stalking ass problem that only a shrink can fix, but me and Trina aren't paid to fix your issues. Go find one. We can't help you."

"Looks to me like we," he responded back to Creed, pointing his finger back and forth between his chest and Creed's, "got ourselves a misunderstanding. See, Trina is beautiful. She's always been since I've been with her. I watch her every day. I follow her to make sure she gets where she needs to be safely, and I even was alone with her in the house today. So you see, she lied to you. Trina is my lady. The only one stalking and in my way is you...Creed. She had to kill your baby because I told her to," he stated with evil painted across his face, "just to make room for mine."

"Man, forget this small talk shit," Creed stated as his blood tortured him inside as it boiled so much that he swung the hammer at the assailant's face. He missed and the guy named Evan raised his knife and sliced Creed's arm open, but Creed caught him right back in the thigh with the hammer as his arm fell in excruciating pain. Creed then leaned forward with his other arm and charged him, grabbing the arm that had the weapon. They both tumbled to the floor.

Trina couldn't stand by and allow her boyfriend to suffer anymore damage without her help, so she reached over and grabbed the hammer that had fallen to the floor. As Creed struggled to keep the man from stabbing him with the knife, Trina rushed over to them both, and as Creed held on to the assailant's arm, she swung. The hammer slammed into the jaw of the man who was somehow fascinated with her, and his arm dropped to the floor, just missing her ankle.

"Gimme that hammer, T," Creed ordered as she fell backwards against the wall while handing it to him. He finally was able to stand tall and then with a deep breath, he leaned in with all his force and slammed the hammer into his knee. "And that's for fuckin' up my knee." Then he took the hammer and crushed his arm. "The same thing goes for my arm, crazy bastard."

Creed kneeled back over, searched the man's pockets, and ended up running into a cell phone. From there, he tossed it to Trina. "Dial the number."

***

"Oh my baby," Trina's mom cried running up to her as Trina sat at the hospital. Her parent's return flight landed on their home turf only hours after they got word of Trina's call on their answering machine which was hours after she called.

Trina stood up, completely shaken by the ordeal that happened at her home, however, she was never happier to see her parents than she was when they stepped off the elevator. "Mom…dad…I'm so glad you're back home. I can't go back there, ma. He tried to kill me."

With tears in her eyes, her mom embraced her while her father walked over and placed his arms around them both. "Baby, what happened? I'm so sorry. Tell me what went wrong?" he asked. "Are you hurt?"

Trina backed away and wiped her eyes. She knew what she was about to tell them wouldn't be good, however, she'd already told the officer that she preferred to tell them the whole truth of the night. Their response couldn't be any worse than a man trying to kill her, so she started, "I threw a party after your flight took off, dad. I thought I'd found out that Jeremy," she began to cry thinking about his body at the bottom of the pool, "wasn't supposed to be back until the party was over to check on me, but he ended up coming. I let a bunch of people come over, but more people than I even knew showed up. This guy was already in the house with me…or he didn't leave or something, mom," she continued, staring into her mom's eyes. "I didn't know this would happen. He killed Grace and Jeremy, dad," she cried, " And he would have killed me if I didn't call Creed. Creed helped me get out of the house, and in the process, he got his knee injured bad, and the guy slashed through his arm." Her watery eyes batted between the both of them as they stood completely still without anything to say. Although stunned, her mother spoke while her father rubbed the graying, well-kept beard on his chin.

"Are you hurt anywhere?"

"No ma'am."

"Where is Creed?"

"Mama, please…"

"Where is Creed?" she asked sternly, refusing to accept anything but the truth.

Trina stared at the floor. "He's in the room."

"Take me to him.

"Take us both to him, baby girl," her father chimed in, and at that point, Trina knew things were different. She immediately looked at the officer, and he walked them down to where Creed's room was located.

Creed was lying there in the bed with a huge bandage covering his arm, an IV drip for pain in his other arm, and his leg held up in a sling. Trina's mother and father were the first to enter the room and speak to the officer, resulting in the officer leaving the room. After the officers left and went down the hallway, appearing to exit, it was then that Trina walked inside the room behind her parents. She found her mother gripping Creed tightly and weeping in his arms, apologizing and repeating the words, "Thank you for saving my daughter." Her father stood there, grabbed his hand, and held on to it as firm as he ever did, but this time, it was in much respect and love.

Trina cried and finally felt relief from her parents' acceptance of her love for Creed.

It turned out that Evan was actually an escaped mental patient who had been institutionalized since the age of fourteen. His full name was Stephen Evans, and he had gained a unique fascination with Trina on social media where her profile was public. He would watch her every day, heavily detailing the times she got up and the times she went to sleep, even her activities in between. He would imagine doing all the things she posted online along with her, and that was his way of escape...until he finally did it. It didn't take him long to find out where she was located because she never hid her location. Wherever she was, she tended to post it and the city was always readily seen. Evans hitched and walked to the place where he could sit and watch her every step of the way, imagining her as his own for six whole months. There was one secret that she nor Creed ever knew. It was Evans who watched Creed finish the fight that led him to going to jail. Evans was the anonymous caller that got him locked up so that he could have Trina all to himself.

"Stephen Evans," a nurse called entering to tend to his injuries after he was transferred to a hospital close to the mental facility from where he escaped years ago. A psychiatrist came in behind her.

"So you're back to join us, Stephen?" his psychiatrist asked in a pleasant welcome back sort of way. "You've been busy."

"My girlfriend...Trina...we plan on having a baby. We made up, and she dumped that boyfriend of hers. Yeah, me and her, when I get better, we'll have a son, and his name will be Evan. Evan Jr. She promised me." His eyes lit up like his face had never been hit with a hammer.

"Isn't this lady you're in love with the same lady that hit you with the hammer?"

"Oh this? People get angry." There was a silence, and Evans looked away. "That's what happens sometimes when people are in love like we are. We do some things," he continued, looking back at the psychiatrist, "that people consider crazy sometimes. I'll take her back. I'm not mad at all."

Four Years Later

"Hey, baby, you're late," Trina greeted her husband of two years as he got ready to go to the job that his father in law got for him soon after the attack, making them not only family but co-workers as well.

"Yeah, I know. Being late to anything won't look too good with my track record." Creed stepped out with the slightest limp left from the attack. He leaned over to kiss their newborn baby girl, and then, walked over and gave her a kiss on the lips. "You taste yummy, babe, and that's all the breakfast I need. I have to go. Pops always has donuts on his desk. I'll sneak in and steal one."

Trina laughed, "Okay! Don't get arrested."

"I won't. Have a good day. I'll call you on my break."

"I love you," she called behind him.

"I love you two, too." He left out.

After Creed accepted the job Trina's dad offered him, for two years he was able to save up enough money, purchase a starter home and then ask for Trina's hand in marriage. Her father couldn't say no to a man that risked his life and saved his only child. Trina's parents gave their blessing, and they were married.

It didn't take long for Trina to become pregnant again and give birth while going to school online.

Her parents were disgusted about her choice of online schooling, however, since the incident, they were far more lenient on her than before. Besides that, she was a grown woman and proved her decision making skills were much clearer in more ways than one over the years. Trina enjoyed being a stay at home mom and wife, and was focused on learning more about business in order to start her own company one day in the near future.

As she sat down on the couch next to her newborn baby girl, she flicked on the television set, lifted her baby from the bassinet, and rocked her back and forth. Her wireless headset was wrapped around her neck, so when her cell phone rang, she had no problem pressing the button with a nice greeting.

"Hello?"

"Hi."

Trina straightened up on the chair and pressed the volume up on the headset because she didn't recognize the voice on the other end. "Hello? Who's speaking?"

"I'm surprised that you don't know me after all this time."

"Well," she continued, placing her child down. The baby began to cry as she released her from her comforting arms. "Shh, baby," she stated, then continued with her conversation on the telephone. "I'm sorry, all this time?"

There was a silence, and when the voice spoke again. "I see we have a baby now, Trina."

Chills ran down her spine that frightened her so much that she snatched her child up like a ragdoll and ran to the bathroom, locking the door tightly. The voice she recognized. She heard the voice of Evan…Stephen Evans. Quickly, she attempted a voice dial of Creed, but for some reason, her phone failed to connect.

"Creed, dial Creed," she continued, but there was only a buzz on the other end. "Oh, Jesus, not again. Not again. I have a baby, Lord, I have a baby!" she screamed, already shaking so much that she laid two towels down in the tub, removed the plug to the drain, and placed her baby down inside for complete safety. "Mama's not gonna let anyone hurt you, baby. Not anyone." She turned to the pipes at the sink and began to unscrew them as fast as she could to use as her only weapon. Then, she moved toward the bathroom door. When she heard nothing, she opened the door and walked into the hallway. She turned to the right, and her cell phone was in the same position on the arm of the chair. She could see the red light from where she stood, notifying her that it was low on charge. Trina then rushed over to it. Before she plugged it into the wall, there was a new message, and she opened it up. It read, *"I will be there soon enough. Don't ever think I've left you alone."*

Trina dropped the phone instantly, and the many wounds from years ago came back to haunt her. She ran to the blinds and shut them all, starting with the living room. Afterwards, she moved to the kitchen and then to the dining room area, double checking to be certain that each window was locked. Her baby girl began to wail from the bathtub which broke her concentration, and she ran down the hall, fighting to get to her child whom she left protected within the confines of an empty tub.

She ran into the bathroom, and when she saw that her baby was safe from all harm, she lifted her up from the tub. However, as she came to an erect stance, the bathroom window was before her and staring back at her was the man she met who tried to take her life – Stephen Evans. He stood there with a smile on his face and no ski mask to hinder her from identifying him.

Trina incidentally fell backwards with the baby wrapped in her arms, screaming at the top of her lungs. She bolted out of the bathroom as soon as she regained her footing and plugged in her cell phone.

"He's here, Creed," she panicked as she fumbled the charger until it finally plugged into the socket. She continued to search the house with her eyes as her daughter lay screaming in her arms. As soon as she connected the phone to the charger, instead of dialing Creed, she dialed emergency.

"Hello, hello! Please send someone here quick. There's a man who was stalking me, and he was looking through my window."

"Ma'am, can you tell me where he is now?"

"No! Dammit, no! He's just outside my house. I need help or he's gonna get in somehow. He's gonna get in. I have a baby," she cried, tears falling atop her child's face as she shook her to try and soothe her from the chaos around her.

"Ma'am, I have an officer on the way."

"One officer? This mother fucker is crazy! He won't go to jail. He's crazy…he already killed my friends, and he wants me."

"What's his name? Can you identify him?"

"Stephen Evans…he told me his name was Evan, but his name is Stephen Evans." Her conversation was interrupted by a steady knock at the door, and even though the operator was still on the line talking, Trina put the phone down and ran her baby back into the crib.

"Here, baby. Mama's gotta kill somebody," she stated firmly through her shakes and tears as she placed a pacifier into her child's mouth. "I love you so much," she cried before bolting to her bedside to retrieve Creed's blade.

She heard the knock once again, and this time it was louder. Walking cautiously toward the door, she glanced through the peephole, but there was no one there. Placing her hand atop the doorknob, she started to turn it slowly, still unable to hear anyone outside the door. Trina took a deep breath, gripped her knife while unwilling to go through the same thing she'd already gone through, and finally swung the door open.

"Excuse me, ma'am." An unfamiliar man stepped into her line of vision from the side of the small porch and without thinking any stable thoughts, Trina swung the knife, stabbing the side of the brick only centimeters away from the man's face, taking a small piece of his skin along with the blade. "Shit, lady!" the man yelled, stumbling back into the bushes that lined the front of the house.

Trina said nothing. She only continued to look at him with confused eyes because the man's face looked nothing like the Evan she remembered. She then stepped outside with the knife held high into the air like she was going to stab him once again, causing the man to fall backwards again into the grass due to his inability to stand back up out of pure shock.

"I just came to hand you a flier, that's it! See!" He then tossed about ten fliers into the air that promoted a fashion show that was to be held at the mall in two weeks. "I got nothing on me. Nothing, lady," he stated as he felt a prick from his face. "You tried to stab me!"

Suddenly, Trina dropped the knife and immediately began apologizing, only then realizing what she'd done to what looked to be an innocent man. As she approached him tearfully apologizing constantly, he heard the sound of sirens.

"You called the cops on me? Ain't no sign out here that says no soliciting? I'm already on probation, lady. I have a fashion show to promote...trying to make a living," he yelled, frustrated. "No, move!" he shouted at Trina again as she reached for his face.

"I didn't know. I thought you were somebody else. I'm sorry," she cried.

"I'm out. Damn," he complained, jumping in his car that was only parked feet from where he stood and drove off. The sirens were still blaring, and Trina rushed back to the porch after picking up all the fliers and her knife. She then closed and locked the door in order to set things back in order before the cops came to the house, placing the knife back at her bedside.

Upon hearing the officer's car outside her home, she quickly picked up her baby and headed toward the front door, terribly frightened of what she'd just done, nearly stabbing an innocent person. At the same time, she was even more confused by her sighting of whom she thought was Evan. She still had proof, however. That proof was in a text message to her phone.

"How you doin', ma'am? We got a message saying there was an intruder at this residence? Are you the owner of the house and the one who placed the phone call to 911?"

Still trembling slightly but trying to remain calm as she glanced unsuspectingly down the road to ensure the man she cut was gone, she replied, "Yes…yes sir. I made the call. I thought I saw a man," she stated as she moved away from the door allowing the officers inside, "standing outside my bathroom window looking right at me. It…it was a man that attacked me years ago, and I thought he was back. I mean, he was staring right at me, officer."

"Okay, calm down," he ordered her as he sensed she was getting more emotional. "I'm gonna go around back. Stay inside here, and when I get back, we'll talk more. Got a description?"

"Yeah…uhm…he's about six feet tall, African American…light skinned and light brown eyes. I didn't see his clothing."

"You can identify him if I get him?"

"Yes, definitely," Trina assured him as she watched him walk outside the door. She stood there impatiently, shaking her baby as if she'd just finish feeding her a bottle, patting her on the back and cuddling her, however, it was more to give herself comfort. Before the officer got back inside, Trina was already sitting on the couch waiting, however, not certain if what she saw was even real. The officer entered the home once again, and he came with no one.

"Ma'am, I saw nothing, no evidence of anyone lurking behind your house nor on the sides of it. One second, please," he paused as he walked away while speaking on his hand held radio.

Trina didn't know what else to do or what else to tell him, so she rushed back to the back, placed her child in the swing, and came back out of the room. She picked up her cell phone and waited until the officer was finished with whatever he was doing pertaining to the call she made. As soon as he placed the radio back on his waist, Trina walked right up to him anxiously, showing him the call that came through to her phone and telling him exactly what was said.

"Yes sir," she stated, pointing to her phone. "This was the call I got…see it. It's unidentified, but it was him. He thinks we have a child together…my child," she exclaimed. "He's a psycho in a mental ward, and his name is Stephen Evans. And look…there's a text message that came with it." As the officer looked on, Trina pulled up the text message that was sent, but doing so resulted in her full out panic. When she revealed it, she immediately didn't know how to explain herself. She looked closer at the message, and she realized that she totally ignored who sent it. It was Creed. Creed sent the message, not Evan. She closed the message.

"I think I made a mistake, officer. I think I did…and I'm sorry. I happened to nearly be killed years ago, and I think I must have imagined or dreamed up…" Trina continued as she cried, placing her hand up against her forehead while holding her head down in shame. The officer only watched as Trina's hair fell down over her face like a blanket, but then he interrupted her tears briefly.

"Sometimes, when cruel and unusual things happen to people, it leaves room for some counseling. If someone attacked you before, it may be a good idea to get some help for the memories or the stress that was left over from it…before you get yourself in some trouble. Are you sure that this was just a case of your mind playing tricks on you?"

"Yes, yes, officer," she nodded. "I'm fine now."

"Listen, I'll take another look around your property, and if I find something in the least bit suspicious, I'll come back to the door. If not, I'll be on my way. Take care of your young one back there and lock up."

She nodded and closed the door behind the officer. Ashamed of herself, she slid down the door and then opened her messages once again. There the message was, just as clear as when she read it the first time... *I will be there soon enough. Don't ever think I've left you alone.*

"It was my imagination," she began to laugh through the tears. "Unbelievable...that phone call...it was probably somebody else, and I had to take it there. Really, Trina? Whoever that was is really gonna think I'm nuts." she teased herself getting up from the floor. "He's locked up in the psych ward. Don't get yourself sent there with him," she mumbled. She, then, texted her husband Creed back with the message, "I'll be waiting on you...and thanks." She'd resolved not to mention anything that happened at the house because she'd rather make good memories in their first home and not bad ones.

Going to warm up her baby's bottle, she heard the police officer's car drive off, and immediately felt relief. Although she still pondered over the telephone call, she pushed it to the back of her mind as possibly mistaking the voice altogether. Many people know her telephone number, and Creed, not being the jealous type, knows that her homeboys, who are now all grown and living it up, periodically call from time to time since the big party just to check on her, courtesy of her father having always put them up to it in the past. Old habits for them never died.

Finally, Trina took in a deep breath, got her nerves back together, chuckled a little bit, and walked down the hallway. With each step, she shoved haunting memories of that dreadful night her friends got killed further back into her mind. Unconsciously, she gripped her baby's bottle tightly to combat that same uneasy feeling that she had when she was just a teenager when she thought she was alone in her parents' home.

As she reached the bedroom door of her child's nursery, her heart leaped for joy as she saw her daughter lifting her legs in the air, trying to touch her toes for the first time.

"Look at you, sweetheart. Daddy's gonna be so proud," she continued, picking her up and sitting in the rocking chair that was located next to the crib. For half of the day, Trina did nothing but play with the baby, until she lost track of time, noticing that it was already past lunch time and Creed hadn't called. Therefore, she got up, leaving her sleeping daughter in the crib once again, so that she could go check her phone for any messages.

On the way to the living room, she stopped inside the bathroom to wash her face off once again and put on a little lip gloss. Trina's knack for keeping herself looking radiant throughout the day hadn't stopped, a lesson she learned from her mother. No matter if it was at night or the day, it was always important to appear ready for anything, even if you're really not. Trina brushed her ponytail back in place, and gave herself a small gargle with some mouthwash before setting back off toward her cell. Before walking out of the bathroom, she stopped to look back at the bathroom window. Then, she smirked. "My mind sure messed me up today."

She exited the bathroom and went directly to her phone which was, at that time, fully charged. "Why didn't Creed call me on his lunch break?" She saw that she had no missed calls nor any new voice mail, however, there was one text message waiting to be read. It was from Creed again, and it read, *"Baby, I won't be able to call you, so I'll see you when I get there. All day meeting, and the group is running late on the deadline. Working with them through lunch."*

"Bummer," Trina stated feeling a bit let down as a result of not being able to talk to Creed as she normally did. Everything had been going better than ever as the years passed, and there wasn't one second that the two were ever apart since fighting for their lives years ago. Because of that, Trina and Creed weren't only lovers in wedlock, but they were also survivors and best friends having already realized that they could make it through anything after having been through too much.

"I guess I'll just start on dinner. Cabbage, yams, ham and rice," she sighed. "A small Thanksgiving meal right before the holiday." She moseyed into the kitchen, pulled out her cutting board, butcher knife, cabbage and warmed up the oven. "By the time he gets home, dinner will be hot, and he will be hungry. I hope this comes out right," she doubted herself referring to the ham. It was her first time making one. Trina wasn't the best cook, but Creed appreciated her effort. Whenever she would completely wreck a meal, however, they would all hop in the car and have a night out...on her, no matter how much Creed would try and wolf the food down. She'd hoped tonight wasn't one of those nights.

By eight o'clock in the evening, all the food was cooked and kept warm by Trina leaving it stove top with the oven on. She peeped out the window, and Creed still wasn't at home, but she knew he was on his way, therefore, she quickly made her way into the bathroom and jumped into the shower.

As the water rinsed the stress from her skin, she smiled when she heard the chime of the alarm signaling the front door had been opened. Because of the aroma sent through the house, she imagined the look on Creed's face as he went sniffling through the kitchen.

"Don't even think about it, babe!" she jokingly yelled through the house. "We eat when you fix my plate and only after then! Besides, I did all the hard labor in there," she laughed. She placed her ear to the shower curtain while she held a big smile on her face awaiting his response, but when she didn't get a reaction, she shrugged her shoulders, turned the water off and stepped out onto the bathroom rug.

Right beside her was the towel, so she ripped it off the hook, and starting with her face, dried off. Afterwards, she wrapped the towel around her body, slid on her footies, and walked curiously out of the bathroom after letting her hair back down.

"Creed, I made a big meal for you, so ..." she stated upbeat, however, when she didn't see Creed in the living room or the kitchen, she glanced over to the front door. It was cracked. "What is he doing? Got me in here talking to myself." She then walked to the door as she twisted her hair, peeked her head out of the door slightly as to not showcase her entire body to any passersby, and checked the driveway. There his car sat, but there was no sign of him. "Creed, baby, where are you?" When he didn't answer, she walked away from the door only to see her phone ringing. It was her father.

"Hello?" she asked, swiftly picking her cell phone up from the coffee table. "Hey, daddy, what's up?"

"Nothing much there, baby girl. I was calling," he started, clearing his throat, "To see just how Creed was doing?"

"How Creed is doing? How about how I'm doing or your brand new granddaughter?" Trina teased with a slight giggle. "As far as Creed, he's outside...somewhere...just pulled up maybe like five minutes ago."

"So he's feeling better?"

She placed her body up against the wall and wiggled her toes as she waited on Creed to walk through the door. "Feeling better? What...was he sick or something at work because he woke up this morning feeling great? Of course, he didn't eat my breakfast but still..." she laughed.

"Not sick?" he asked.

"No, dad, why?"

"He didn't even show up to work today that's why. He uh...yeah...here it is. He sent me a text message, and I'm just checking up on him after we counted him out today. It says he had something like an upset stomach that felt like the flu…"

Trina's ears went deaf as she lifted her eyes at the front door, pondering her father's words. Creed never made it to work? Her heart began to race as her breathing became erratic, struggling with thoughts of what she'd convinced herself against earlier. Those vivid realities of the phone call she'd received, the text message and even his face…the face of the man who introduced himself to her as Evan in the grocery store years back. It wasn't her imagination. It was real. It was all real, and he was here.

Tears began to fall down Trina's face once again as an awesome fear disturbed her ability to run. Her dad's continuous calls for her on the other end of the phone went unanswered as she turned to face the carpeted hallway. Everything around her started to tumble inward as she felt no escape while walking down the narrow corridor. Her eyes turned so fast from one side of the hallway to the other that they appeared to move faster than a twitch as her legs carried her ever so slowly. Quakes began to fill her stomach, quakes that were so powerful that her entire body began to shake uncontrollably.

The light from the bathroom shined a wonderful light into one section of the hallway, but beyond that small section, there was nothing more than darkness. She moaned in the shakiest whisper, "Creed," but her faint call brought no relief as she took more steps toward her bedroom. As she turned to look inside, there was only darkness, the bathroom light only casting a tender glow across the bed. "Creed," she whimpered once again, and still nothing.

"Shh…" a voice came, breaking her trance from the unknowns of the darkness. It came from directly behind her. The sound was coming from her baby's nursery. Trina's entire body caved in, taking her perfect posture along with it, as her hands gripped her head while the cell phone dropped to the floor. She began to moan horribly as she turned her body around slowly to the voice she couldn't label as Creed's.

Her breathing became heavier, as a woman who had possibly just lost her only child; a breathing of terror as she watched a man sitting on her rocking chair erect, going back and forth in the pitch black. She reached over and turned on the light, and there he was, holding her brand new precious baby on his shoulder with blood covering his hands as he patted her on the back while she continued to suck her pacifier. He stroked her back as the blood stained her white pajamas, and then he smiled.

"I told you I would never leave you alone."

The last thing her father heard on the other end of the cell phone was his only daughter screaming and his grandbaby crying. Creed was nowhere to be found.

THE END

I Thought I Was Alone 2

"That's not funny, Diana," she smirked at her best friend in the entire universe. They'd been friends since kindergarten, and since they started college, they felt they were starting all over again.

"Stop what, Ayana?" she stated in her Puerto Rican accent while giving her a nudge. "You know you like him. Go talk to him," she pushed, fluffing her dark brown hair around her left shoulder. "We're in college, girl. It's time to let loose a bit." She fell atop her twin bed feeling like she'd made it for the first time in her life. "You just don't know what it feels like, Ayana, to not have to share your life with siblings. My folks struggled so much to get me here for this very moment, and if it wasn't for your awesome father and his mega wallet, I would have nowhere to stay but in that freshman residence hall. I heard it was the worst."

"Didn't my father tell you not to mention that again, Diana? Look," she stated, going over to sit beside her on the bed. "We're just like sisters, and he knew how important it was for you to be with me in college. We both got in after graduating and spending our whole lives together, so when he asked me what I wanted as a gift, he knew it would be my best friend to live with me in this two bedroom little cottage. It's nice, huh? We're probably like the only freshmen to actually have our own...really own house."

"Thanks so much, Ayana. You're like my sister...even if I am Puerto Rican."

"They have black Puerto Ricans, too. You just came out as the lighter version," she laughed. "No one would be able to tell the difference if you sat out in the sun a bit. You'd look just as African American as I am. Sisters for life?" she said wiggling her pinky finger.

"Sisters for life!" Diana confirmed, shaking her pinky finger with Ayana's. Then, she stopped and snatched Ayana toward the window by the wrist. "Oh, look, look. He's coming back again," Diana squealed. "Hey you!" she yelled from the window.

"Diana!" Ayana called, growing embarrassed by the second because when she turned to face the window once again, the guy Diana called Mr. Hey You was looking back in her face while Diana sat ducked beneath the window pane. "You ass," Ayana whispered as she slowly backed away from the window, kicking Diana in the leg as she left the room, leaving her on the floor giggling until her stomach was in knots.

Ayana walked across to her bedroom, still in disbelief about how Diana put her on the spot in front of the first guy she said was cute. The last thing Ayana wanted to be known for was being a flirt, especially as it was the first weekend on campus before classes started. She began to open one of the last boxes that she brought from home that contained a photo album and framed pictures of her family that lived about an hour away. She hadn't looked in the photo album much when she lived with her family, but now that she was on her own, she missed them as if she were away for a lifetime.

As she pulled the photo album from the box, she opened the album to find all the experiences she'd loved one moment in time. It made her look around at her present time and soak everything in before taking another look at the rest of the photos. There were many pictures of her father and mother celebrating with her during birthdays and Christmas, Easter and even on vacations. As she continued turning the pages, she ran into pictures of herself having a blast at an amusement park with her cousins. One of the cousins in the picture was her older cousin Trina, and as soon as she saw the photo, she shut the book, shoving it back into the box.

Trina was the closest cousin that Ayana had ever had. She taught her to apply make-up, do manicures and pedicures which she figured would get her side money while in college instead of depending on her dad's money all the time. Trina even taught her to entertain. She remembered that Trina would sometimes be the only audience she had as she recited her poetry…while everyone else seemed uninterested. It was always Trina who pushed her and even critiqued her poetry which built Ayana's confidence. Since Trina had been placed in temporary psychiatric care, things hadn't been the same. Watching her child be murdered was something that Trina still couldn't move beyond and probably never will, but then again, it had only been six months. They still hadn't found the body of her husband, and the man who killed him wouldn't reveal where he put the body. All they knew was that he was dead.

Ayana laid back onto her bed, pulled her cell phone out of her back pocket and called her father. She got no answer, so she turned over and ended up taking a short nap until waking up only an hour later to start getting ready for a party later on that night.

**

"So, how do I look?" Ayana asked as she twisted from left to right in her skin tight mini-dress.

"You look good…just not better than me. See," Diana turned around to show her body off in not just a skin tight mini just like her best friend, but her back was completely out, leaving not much to the imagination.

"Are you serious? Girl, this is our first night out together at this university. Are you sure you want to go like that...back all out and everything? There could be weirdos..."

"They won't be any weirder than me, Ayana," she stated with certainty, allowing her luscious locks to flow down over her shoulders. Diana wasn't the innocent type by far, but she wasn't exactly promiscuous either. She'd had her share of boyfriends and with that came plenty rumors. The fact still remained that she was under four when it came to who she'd been with, and that was in a five year time span. She started early. "What?" she asked although knowing full well why Ayana's jaw was still dropped. "Have you never seen a back before? I look good, girl," she stated, twisting around in the mirror. "We're going to be the two hottest ladies at the party, now aren't we?"

Ayana finally laughed as she walked over to her best friend and agreed. "Hell yeah we will be. Let's go." She stared at Diana one more time. "You still could have saved that for another time. First impressions."

"Well, let the guys impress me," she smiled as she led the way out of the front door while Ayana shook her head following behind, double checking the door behind her. Instead of driving, they walked. The party wasn't too far away, and they wanted to soak everything in.

The party was packed by the time they arrived, and it was the atmosphere the two college freshmen were looking for in order to meet others easier, since they lived a short distance away from the dormitories where most other freshmen lived. They were surrounded by upperclassmen where they lived, and although not intimidated in the least, they did want the feel of being with those who just left high school and entered into this brand new world.

As they approached the other side of the room, Ayana felt her cell phone vibrate. She didn't look into her clutch immediately, assuming that it was her father calling to check on her. She'd made mention that she and Diana were going to have a night out together the Saturday before the first day of classes, so it was only natural for her father to feel nervous.

"Diana, let me answer my phone real quick. Stop right here," she requested, grabbing Diana by the wrist. "I know it's dad, so I want to let him know I'm okay. He's overprotective ever since…"

"You don't have to tell me anything. That was your cousin, girl. It was scary. Don't remind me. It'll make anyone watch their back."

"Hello?" Ayana answered as she plugged up her other ear with her finger to block out the music coming from the speakers. Diana was doing the usual pull-the-best-man-in-the-house stance, but Ayana wasn't too concerned about pulling a boyfriend as much as she was on having some innocent fun for the night and getting to know the campus a bit better on Sunday.

"Ayana?" the voice on the other end called. "Ayana, are you there?"

"Oh my goodness. Is this you, Trina?" she asked, surprised to hear her first cousin calling. She pulled the phone away from her ear to view the caller ID which stated her parents' home, and then put it back to her ear. "Trina it is you! What are you doing at my parent's house tonight? Is everything okay?" Ayana's nerves began to go into a frenzy until Trina stopped her.

"Slow down, baby cousin," she laughed. "I'm finally able to get out of the house now…slowly, but yeah…I'm able to visit now. One step at a time. Your dad told me that he was about to call and check on you, and I told him that I would do the honors. I'm proud of you, Ayana. You're doing something that I never did…" she continued going into a silence before picking up her tone again, "so I suppose I will live through you."

"Have you ever thought about…"

"No, Ayana. I haven't. I still want my own business, you know. My psychiatrist told me that I can still do it, but you know…"

"Yeah, yeah," Ayana interrupted, not wanting to dampen the conversation or her festive mood. "Well, I'm at a party right now, trying to meet new people, so I will call you back as soon as I'm back home at about two o'clock in the morning or so. Will you still be there, or do you finally have a number where I can call you directly?"

"I'll crash here tonight…hang out and talk trash about you," Trina laughed. "Take care of yourself, and we'll be by the phone. Well, I'll be by the phone because your folks can't hang," she laughed. "They've never been able to. And, yes, I do have my own number again, so I'll text it to you."

"Later…and love you." Ayana kissed the phone and then put it back in her clutch. "That was Trina!" she said in shock.

"Trina?" Diana looked back surprised. "Seriously? How is she?"

"She's fine. At least she sounds like she's doing better. It's only been six months since she lost baby Zoe and her husband Creed to that lunatic. What's unfair about it though is that the craze is still alive and well, sitting up pretty in the insane asylum...and you know they never found Creed. She's definitely a fighter though."

"After being stabbed twenty times, I would say so. It's just a shame her husband and newborn didn't make it." Quickly, Diana felt she'd said too much and apologized for saying it. Ayana didn't mind, however.

"It's fine, Diana," she stated as she thought about her late newborn baby cousin, having been alive only weeks before she was taken away. "He'll get what he deserves in the long run. Anyway," she continued, shaking the thoughts of her cousin's attack away, "Let's get this party started!" she shouted, pulling Diana on the dance floor with her. The place was full, but no one was dancing, and the one thing Ayana loved to do was dance. She didn't mind being the center of attention at all when it came to the dance floor, and neither did Diana.

They were the first ladies on the dance floor, and by the end of the night, everyone had taken at least three or four laps around the dance floor just as they did. The night was amazing, and on top of that, they met many people. For the most part, their night came to a close with extreme excitement for the first day of classes, and as they walked out of the party, the night got even better for one of them.

"Ayana, is that the guy from earlier today behind us?"

"I don't know. Why?"

"Well, if you would turn around, it looks like he's trying to get your attention."

"What?" Ayana asked confused, until she turned around and saw exactly who Diana was talking about. Immediately, she spun back around, completely faced forward and changed her gait. Diana then looked at her strangely.

"Uhm, why are you suddenly walking like that...like a stick is stuck up your butt and you're ballet dancing?"

"Shut up, Diana. I'm nervous as hell that's why. Dang, I can't believe this," Ayana stated embarrassed.

"Well, you need to relax and loosen up that swag in your back and let those butt cheeks loosen up a bit along with it because he's coming," she stated, turning back around and waving. "And it looks like he's not coming for me because he's headed to your side."

"Diana! Waving...really? Did you have to..."

"Excuse me," a strong, deep voice called that sounded like it was five feet behind her. At first Ayana didn't turn around, but then she heard him call again, so she stopped. However, when she turned around, she didn't expect him to be so close to her, within ten inches. Diana continued walking slowly, wandering a little further down the road by a lone tree with the university's colors painted on the bark.

"Are you talking to me?" Ayana asked in one of her moments where she had nothing highly intelligent to say.

"Of course I'm talking to you. Wasn't that you up there in the window of that house that called me earlier this morning when I was walking by?" His eyes were a must to stare into as the night light shown them as a nice dark chocolate, just like his skin. He was the most perfected man on campus that Ayana had seen since she set foot in her new place of residence, and deep inside, she hoped he didn't live far from away from her dwelling.

"Well, sort of. I was looking, but my friend," Ayana explained, turning back to point towards Diana, "she was the one who called you."

"My mistake. I guess I better go and see what's up with…" he stated, pretending to make his way over to Diana who was busy taking off her heels.

Ayana placed her body in front of his before he got too far. "Oh no you don't," she smiled, understanding that he was just joking.

"I was just kidding around with you."

"I know."

"So…is this your first year, or did you transfer in from somewhere else? I'm Dean by the way, and your name is?"

"I'm Ayana, and yes," she took a deep breath staring around at the campus and then back at him. "This is my very first year. Are you an antique around campus or are you joining me on this adventure?"

"Antique?" he laughed. "Are you on your way back to your house?"

"Yes," she hesitated being that she didn't know Dean well at all. "I am actually. It's late, and we have no idea where else to go."

"I'm on the way back, too, so if you don't mind, this junior would like to drive you back. You two really should think twice about walking out here without more than five people on your way back that way. Can't be too safe this late, or should I say early in the morning."

"Why is that? I see everyone else out here walking back in couples."

"But they live on the campus. We're right outside. I shouldn't say outside, but we share with the general public. These others have a hop and a skip while they're all going in the same direction. You…well we…we turn off. Different areas are just a bit safer than others."

"We don't live in a safe spot?"

"No spot is too safe for two ladies, dressed like you and your friend. So come on, what do you say?" He pulled out his wallet. "Take my ID, my watch, and as a matter of fact, take my whole wallet. It's empty. School costs money."

Ayana laughed. That was the first good sign from Dean besides his looks that she'd come across. He seemed to have a great sense of humor and to tag along with that a sense of humbleness as well. Ayana glanced back at Diana, then back at him as she thought about the ride back. "Let me take a rain check."

"I promise to you, I'm not a killer. I just want you to get home safe."

"Is that all?"

"And get to chat with you a bit once your friend goes inside," he smiled. "I can walk you though, but damn, I would hate to have to walk all the way back over here just to get my car tonight, especially when we live right next to each other." Ayana stood there silently pondering what to do, and then he handed her his car keys. "You drive."

She smiled, taking the keys, "Thanks...and thanks for the ride."

"Anything to make you feel better. You can pat me down, but that would look freaky as hell out here, don't you think?"

Ayana shook her head and giggled once again. "Diana, come on," she called, lifting the keys up in the air. "We have a ride back." Diana turned away from the tree, faced her and then put her thumbs up.

"As long as he's not crazy, I'll ride, too." Then she started walking toward them, staring him directly in the face. "Don't let us have to cut your ass now...because we will."

"Diana, really? Did you really have to say that?" Ayana shook her head. Then she glanced back at the well built, six feet two young man with absolutely no money and said, "Show me the way to your car."

"Look no further."

Ayana looked around the street, but didn't see a car. "What? Your car is out here somewhere?" She continued to scan around the crowd of people continuing to exit the party, but she didn't see any car.

"Wait one second. Okay, now look," Dean stated as he reached over and took Ayana by the hand ever so gently, causing her to turn to the spectacle of a car that was revealed when the crowd migrated from concealing it on the street. "Most people park in the back, and that's why you don't see many cars parked out here where mine is. I hate fighting for something when I can make the right one mine right away," he spoke, admiring a blushing Ayana. "And I'm talking about the parking space."

"Smart," Ayana replied, knowing full well that he was flirting with her. That was when Diana turned around, spoiling the moment with bad timing and awful humor.

"Is it this one over here," she pointed, "The one with the dent on the back?" she giggled, poking fun at the obvious sign of a car accident. "It may be a good thing that you have the keys, Ayana."

Dean glanced down at Ayana. "I see your friend is full of jokes. It must be fun to have her around."

"I'm sorry about her. She really does like to have fun."

"I can tell. Let's get outta here."

They both catch up to Diana who had already made her way to the only car left on the road. She had positioned herself to hop into the backseat of the silver colored Saturn with the dent in the back while Ayana opened the driver's side door. Once she got inside, she took a whiff of the freshly scrubbed down scent of the car, and she even spotted the bottled water sitting in the cup holder. It made her feel more at ease as she opened the doors with the automatic lock. At least she knew he was clean and made it a habit to stay hydrated. As he was talking to her, she even smelled his breath which wasn't stained with the strong odor of alcohol. It was the unspoken that Ayana was mostly concerned with when it came down to living on her own for the first time. Her dad drilled it into her head before she left.

"Took you long enough, Ayana. Wow," she complained as she sat down in the backseat and shut the door, "the front of my toes feel like a fifty pound dumbbell is rolling back and forth into them. The throbbing is killing me."

"Is that what heels do to you?" Dean asked as he took a seat in the passenger's side. He glanced at Ayana who hesitated about putting the keys into the ignition. "You do know how to drive, right?"

"Yeah...sorry." She felt guilty about being so paranoid towards him and causing the whole driver shuffle. "I'm just..."

"Smart as hell. Apology not accepted. Let's go," Diana interjected, realizing that most people could easily place Ayana in a guilt trip. Diana was usually the person to get her out of her guilt trip as soon as it started because she believed in doing and saying what was necessary at all times. Apologizing for it was like nurturing the beast and giving it another stab at you.

Ayana rolled her eyes at Diana, and Dean just chuckled at her slick tongue. Finally, she started the car and drove off.

"Generally, after a party, most of us head out to get something to eat, like at a pancake house or something," Dean stated to make light conversation. There was tension in the air, and he didn't quite know why but figured it was because the ladies were in a strange place with him as the strange person.

"Oh...do you want to go over to where they are? You have no money though," she giggled.

"I didn't say I didn't have any money. You plugged that in for me," he laughed. At that, he pulled out about three twenty dollar bills from his front right pocket. "The definition of pocket change. Always have some on you as my father would always say. Wallet is bill money."

"I see. My mistake."

"You two hungry?" he asked and watched them nod. "Let's make that happen then. Turn left up here, get in the right lane and make a sharp right again. We'll be there. You know the restaurant two blocks down from us?"

"Are you talking about the restaurant with the big pancake smiley face on the sign that's shaped like a flat egg?" Ayana asked.

"Yeah, that's the place. How did you guess?"

"Well, for one, it stands out like a sore thumb among all the other fancy buildings around it. Number two, although it stands out painfully, it looks like they can burn!"

"Get ready to gain some weight, but hey, instead of eating inside, " he started, turning to face her. "Let's get some carry out. Pull up to the drive through if you don't mind, and that way, we can chill a little bit."

"I know what that means. Whatever," Diana sighed. "I will chill in the house alone tonight while you two chat it up together. The typical third wheel experience." She then leaned up into the middle of the front seats. "Don't get it twisted though. This is my sister here. I will be memorizing these tags before I go inside." She then tapped him on the shoulder. "Thanks for the meal…with your pocket change."

"And you like this girl?" he asked Ayana jokingly.

"Love her," Ayana answered as she pulled up to the drive-thru which already had a backed up line. As soon as they rode up to the drive-thru menu, every food item had a nickname, but there was a picture beside it to let you know exactly what it was that was being purchased. Everything looked great to Ayana and Diana, but they decided to play it safe and follow Dean's lead. He ordered basic pancakes with strawberries, and they followed suit. They then headed back to the house after situating the food, and as soon as they pulled into the driveway, it wasn't three full seconds before Diana jumped out of the backseat, ran to the back of the car, memorized the tags like she swore she would do, and skipped inside, saying bye-bye with her hand straight up in the air.

"Your friend is a trip, Ayana."

"She's more like my sister. I've known her for my whole life just about. We started school together, and now we're here," she stated, sticking the straw down her cup and taking a sip of the soda that came with her pancakes. It didn't go together with the pancakes, but breakfast in the middle of the night wasn't exactly the norm for Ayana either.

"No kidding. I'm a loner. I don't do the tight friend thing much nor have I ever. I socialize with many people, but I tend to be best alone."

"I see that…from the fact that you left the party all by yourself. It's funny that I didn't even see you in there."

"I saw you though," he responded. "Who could miss you?"

Ayana blushed, and with him staring at her like he wanted to lick her down, she felt uneasy about eating. Therefore, she took another sip of her drink to calm down. Dean was fine, and she honestly didn't know what to do with this upperclassman at all. She'd only dated two boys in school, and just being there with him made her feel pushed into a more mature state.

"How old are you by the way?" she asked to cut the sexual tension that she was beginning to feel.

"I'm twenty-three. I started school at twenty. I wanted to work a little bit first, you know, get my hands wet in my field and save up some."

"What field is that?"

"Well," he said taking a deep breath and taking a bite of his pancakes. "I wanted to be certain it was what I wanted to do before I wasted my time in a career in sports medicine."

"Really? That sounds interesting, and that was a smart thing to do."

"What about you? What are you planning to study?"

"English. I want to become a lawyer and a writer all at the same time. More a writer than anything, but it made sense to study law along with it just in case my skills behind the pen don't work out so well."

"So, in other words, law is a second love."

"Something like that. My father's a judge."

"Oh, it's like that!"

"Yeah," she laughed. "It's like that. Law is in the blood."

"Well, I suppose it's time for me to go," he sighed, closing up his food.

"Really?" Ayana said in shock. "Just because my father's a judge. I am eighteen," she stressed.

Dean laughed. "Well, that's good. So do I need to ask you for one," he asked leaning over to her as his voice changed from joking to passionate, "or will you give it to me?"

She knew he meant a kiss, and she didn't mind giving him a kiss at all. She was highly attracted to him, from the physical all the way through to his conversation, no matter how light it was. This was her very first real experience with a grown man, and even though she was eighteen and legal, she still very much felt like a child…a teen.

He didn't allow Ayana to lean over in the car seat and give him a kiss which caught her by surprise. Instead, he got out of the car, walked over to the driver's side and let her out, guiding her with his hand. She noticed him taking a look at her body in the skin tight dress she decided to wear that night, and she also checked him over, unable to see what was underneath his clothes. However, as he leaned over to place his lips against hers, there was no denying this muscular frame as she placed her hand on his stomach and then moved it further up his chest and then his neck.

His grip was light around her waist, and just as his lips touched her lips, there was a sound from the window of the house.

"Don't even try it! I see you."

It was Diana. She wasn't able to be seen, but she could see them. This made Dean and Ayana laugh out loud, but that was when he took her by the hand to start a stroll in the grass. As they were walking away, Diana shouted again.

"I can still see you! Ten minutes!"

"Diana's wild," he said, holding her hand gently. "At least she looks out for you."

"All the time. I do the same for her. Anyone who takes me, takes her, too."

As soon as they were far enough from the window, they started where they left off…with no interruptions. Ayana's heart had already been penetrated, and she fell for Dean so fast that she didn't even know why. All she knew was that he felt good in her arms, and he made her feel like she was the most beautiful girl on campus. In the middle of their kiss, she pulled away, but he stayed put, staring back into her eyes.

"Do you have a girlfriend?" Ayana asked.

"Are you seeing someone?" Then, he looked away at the empty street, and then back at her. "It's not that it matters if you are or not, though, Ayana. I like you…with or without you having a boyfriend. But to answer your question, no. No, I don't have a girlfriend."

"So you would still be here with me if you knew I had a boyfriend?"

"I mean, you're breaking up with him tonight, so it doesn't really matter," he grinned. "I'll even tell you what to say so he won't feel so bad," he stated cockily.

"Oh really?" Ayana smirked.

"Yeah, really," he said, kissing her again, but this time down her neck. "I don't even need you to tell me if you have one or not. When I see you, you're with me…if that's alright with you? I think that'll be alright, don't you?"

Ayana moved his body back just a little, looked him in his brown eyes, and responded affirmatively, "I guess, I'll be seeing you every day then, huh, because I'm single."

"Hell yeah." He reached in and gave her a nice hug, and Ayana hugged him back. Then, he took her hand once again, and walked her back to the front of her small house , wanting to keep to Diana's ten minute schedule. "Here's my number, Ayana," he smiled, pulling something from his pocket.

"What's so funny?"

"I'm laughing because I wrote it down on this napkin at the party because I knew I would be giving it to you tonight. Tomorrow we can get together again. I live right there." He pointed further down the road to another house that Ayana could barely see.

"That close?"

"What? You wanna come on over?" he suggested in a kidding fashion. "Roommate's gone. He's gonna be out for a while."

"Not tonight. We'll take it slowly, but thanks for everything."

"You're welcome. I was just kidding around. We will never do anything you don't want to do. Like I told you before, I won't hurt you purposely. I'm just not that kind of guy."

"Thanks again. I'll call you, but don't you want my number?"

"I found out that if a woman likes you, she'll do most of the calling. I'll do most of the answering... that is if I like her just as much."

"Well, how will you know it's me?" she asked walking off.

"I'll know. Lock up, beautiful." He stood outside as he waited patiently for Ayana to go inside. When she closed the door, he got into his car, and drove down the road to his place.

Ayana dropped her keys on the table and placed her food on the sofa. "Why did you leave the door unlocked, Diana? Geez! Just because I'm outside doesn't mean anything. We promised that we would always lock up. Never know who's around here. I mean, what if I was attacked or something…with Dean?" She kicked off her shoes, flicked on the television, and sat down to gobble her food down. Dean was right about the food. It was delicious, and Ayana wasted no time filling her empty gut before hitting the sack.

"Diana!" she called, but got no answer. "She must be knocked out already. So much for looking out for me," she said to herself as she stretched out on the couch to get comfortable. "Gosh, I'm tired." She wanted to eat more, but the bed was calling her. Therefore, she got up, placed the food in the refrigerator, and headed back to her room, knocking on Diana's room door as she passed by. "Goodnight! I guess I'll tell you about it in the morning then, huh?" Still, no answer, so Ayana walked into the bathroom, undressed and jumped into the shower. Before turning on the water, she noticed that it hadn't been turned on before she jumped in. That wasn't like Diana. She always showered, sometimes three times a day in between her workouts twice a day. They would be quick, but she would always get them in, especially before bedtime.

"Wow, she left it to me tonight." Quickly, Ayana jumped inside the shower allowed the water to pound her body. Exhausted, she didn't stay in the shower long. After about ten minutes, she stepped out and grabbed the towel on the wall. She continued to think about her night with Diana and ending it with a potential steady boyfriend in Dean. Then, she headed toward her bedroom until she saw that Diana's door was cracked open. "Diana?" she called, but she didn't get an answer. "Girl, hey, I thought you were asleep," she stated as she waltzed inside to an room and empty bed. "Diana, come on, girl. Where are you? Stop acting like a ghost."

She walked out of the room and dragged her feet into the living area, but to her surprise, there was no Diana. "Diana?" She turned around. "See, you play too much. Where are you, Diana? This place is but so big. You can't hide."

Ayana searched everywhere in the house, including under the beds and in the closets, behind the doors and even in the cabinets. When she went back into Diana's room, she noticed the food from the pancake place wasn't eaten, the container completely full. "What?" she asked herself silently. Then, she ran into her room, slid on some jeans and a T-Shirt to only turn back around and run outside.

"Diana!" she called, but still no answer from her friend, and she began to worry. The driveway to the house curved toward the side of the house right in front of Diana's room window, and then, connected to the driveway, there was a narrow cobblestone walkway that led to the front door. As she stepped down onto the walkway and around the side of the house to the driveway, her car was gone. "The hell?" she continued, confused as she rushed further onto the empty driveway, but then stopped as she remembered her father's words to never walk out of the house leaving the door open behind her. Suddenly, she turned back toward the front door, walked back inside, and locked it. Then, she walked back into her bedroom.

"I'll call her," Ayana prompted herself as she started to feel paranoid. Diana was full of tricks and games, but this one was beyond normal. Ayana grabbed her phone and dialed. The phone began to ring...in Diana's room.

Anxiety filled every part of her body as she listened to the phone ring, and a cold chill ran down her spine as she felt something had gone terribly wrong. She slowly rose up from her bed. "Diana, this shit isn't funny. I'm tired, and jokes are pretty damn lame right now. Just show yourself so I can get some sleep. It's not like I'm happy right now. You even moved the car, Diana? That's too damn far. Where is it, on the other side of the house...behind the house?"

Nothing but silence answered her as she crept toward her bedroom's doorway, staring diagonally across the hall into Diana's room. A stroke of fear swept through her veins, causing her to become motionless. The darkness surrounded her like a suffocating blanket, and immediately, she began to lose her breath. She listened for any crack in the floor or sound that didn't belong with her. Then, she turned to stare into the living room once again, but this time, it appeared like a vast disturbance, as if something unseen was out of order. She stepped out into the hallway and called her friend once more.

"Diana?"

**

"Get me out of here!" Diana screamed as she kicked forcefully in an attempt to alert anyone as the car drove down the road. She'd just left the bathroom, and before she even had a chance to eat the food that Dean bought her, it happened. It only took what felt like seconds. It all happened so fast.

She'd walked into the house, and she didn't even turn on any lights because she was used to walking in the dark. It was the way she grew up. Poor people didn't turn on lights unless they had to do so because of the electric bill. That was what the windows were for. When it got dark, it was always time to wind down. One light was allowed, and it was in the living room. It was there that her family would congregate until bedtime.

After going into the bathroom for a quick second, she'd just walked to the window, shouted at Ayana who was about to lay what she considered a nice one on Dean, and then went to her closet to hang up her dress after quickly removing it. She reached up for a hanger, and there he was, staring back at her. Before she could swing or scream, he'd grabbed her by her neck and squeezed tightly, forcing her inside the closet to land right up against his chest. His breath punched against her face as it forced its way out of the black mask that covered anything identifiable about his face. Diana panicked, her hands jolting from one side of the closet to the other in an attempt to grab something that would help her launch away from him. She could find nothing, and his hand went over her mouth while something rigid poked at her side. She shook in fright but listened to him carefully as he whispered in her ear.

"Shhhh…now let's walk and lock your room door."

Tears flowed down her face, and her once elated body turned limp, nearly falling to the floor as she recalled what she'd yelled out the window moments earlier. Ten minutes. He'd been watching her the whole time, and he knew someone else was coming inside.

From there, he shoved her out of the closet, and her weeping eyes met the window with hope that Ayana could see her. She thought to scream but couldn't because what she thought was a knife became a pistol aimed directly at her skull. Quivers that shook like rapids in a full body of rushing water dominated her lips as she couldn't stop them from their horrible tremors. She then walked slowly to the door, imagining a bullet attacking and taking the only life she'd ever known from her in only seconds. Her hand reached for the knob of her bedroom door, and regretfully, she turned the lock, securing her fate with the man that had a gun to her head.

"Please," she whimpered, but he reached back with all his force and slapped her in the back of her head. In the next second, he covered her mouth and took her to the floor.

"Shhh…" he breathed his putrid breath into her ear as Diana recognized Ayana's voice calling her from the front door. She dared not make a sound while her eyes peeled open in the darkness, terrified of what would not only happen to her but to Ayana.

"Why did you leave the door unlocked, Diana? Geez! Just because I'm outside…" called Ayana from the front of the house, and Diana froze stiffly inside the arms of the intruder when she heard Ayana say the door was unlocked. There she lay, with only her bra and underwear on, in the arms of a man who would kill her if she made one false move. She listened as her eyes shifted from left to right as she tried to trace Ayana's movement through the house. She wasn't familiar with the cracks in the floor or the sound of the walls when there was motion, but as more seconds passed by, she didn't have to be. Ayana was at her room door, and the man had her in a headlock with the pistol directly inside her mouth.

His face was pressed against hers, and sweat began to pour down Diana's neck as she struggled to remain calm. Her fingernails dug into the carpet as she fought to stay alive. With a racing pulse, she squeezed her eyes tightly and prayed that Ayana would sense something was wrong and walk back out of the house to get help. But it didn't happen that way. Ayana called her name but proceeded to the bathroom to take a shower. When the water came on, Diana was forced to put on some clothing and remain as quiet as a mouse. She'd ended up reaching for some sweaty clothes she'd used to work out in, and while he stood there with the barrel of a loaded gun to her face, she put them on. The next move was walking her into the hallway with a gun to her back.

Diana glanced at the bathroom door, and all she saw was the rectangular outline of light that shown via the outer cracks. Ayana's name was on the tip of her tongue, and the intruder knew it which was why he shoved her in the opposite direction which was toward the front door. She was being taken at gunpoint, and it was at that moment she turned toward him again and silently pleaded to be released.

"I will do anything, just don't kill me," she wept, hoping that Ayana would just open the bathroom door or turn off the shower, so that she could fight back. It was the perfect timing for there to be two against one because unlike minutes earlier, there was no locked door preventing Ayana from helping her. She knew they could take him because a bullet could only shoot one person at a time. Even if shot, Diana was betting on the odds that neither herself nor Ayana would die from the wound.

"Please," she continued to beg, folding her hands at her face and walking backwards until her body hit the front door.

"Turn around and walk." After ordering her out of the front door, he caused her to stall as he lifted a set of car keys from his pocket. She'd left them on the bed in plain view.

"No, no, no…" she began to weep, but he slapped her in the face and immediately jolted her body up straight as he heard the water turn off in the shower. He then shoved her out of the front door. They were at the car in no time. He forced her in the trunk, slammed it shut, and drove, being missed by Ayana in a matter of minutes.

**

Dean's phone number sat on the couch exactly where she left it. Reaching forward, Ayana immediately turned on the hallway light along with her room light. She was growing even more terrified, and having the small home lit gave her comfort as she listened to Diana's voicemail prompts. She glanced into Diana's room once again and then ran in horror toward the living room couch, her thoughts causing overwhelming distress. As soon as she reached the couch, she dialed Dean, the only other person she knew to contact at the school. After three rings, it picked up.

"Ayana," he answered, proving to her that he would know it was her on the other end when she called.

"Hey, Dean. Yeah, it's me," she spoke, staring at her surroundings as if it had eyes and ears looking and listening to her. "I see you did get it right the first time," she continued, attempting to sound relaxed when in reality, she was severely spooked by the unknown. Her eyes remained glued to the hallway, and then she walked over to the kitchen to grab the only silverware she shoved in the drawer – forks. It was the only weapon she had besides her hands, feet, and teeth.

"Oh, you were testing me? No need to do that, baby," he said taking a deep breath that sounded like he was stretching while lying in the bed. "You got something on your mind?"

"Well…," she responded, quickly going back over to the blinds to see if car lights were shining from the side of the house. There weren't any, so she continued to reveal her situation slowly. "Did you notice anything or like…"

"Like what?"

"I know it's weird, but Diana isn't here."

"What do you mean she's not there? I just dropped you both off."

"I know, but…well, the car is gone, but she would never leave without telling me she's going somewhere, I mean, not in the middle of the night like this. I mean, it's *my* car. We share it and all that, and she can drive it, but… she just doesn't do that. Plus, she was asleep when I came in."

"You didn't see her leave?"

"No. I mean, I came inside, took a quick shower, but when I came out of the bathroom, she was gone. I mean, Dean," she sighed frustrated, "Her food wasn't even eaten. It's on the bed completely cold!" Ayana got up and went through the whole motion of what she did when she went into the the house. "She'd left the door unlocked, and I know we walked off, but it was only ten minutes. I walked by her bedroom door, but it was locked. I figured she was asleep."

"So you didn't see her?"

105

"No, but her door was locked." Her voice accidentally cracked, and it became evident to Dean that Ayana was feeling worse than what she let on.

"Look, lemme get dressed, and I'll come back over there real quick until she gets back. I'm sure it's nothing. Lock up, and I'll be there." He heard her crying. "Ayana, listen," he said softly in order to help her calm down. "It's fine. She's fine."

"Yeah," Ayana responded and then quickly ended the call. She placed her phone down and stared back down the hallway with the fork in a ready to stab position. She started to move down the hallway slowly. The lights were on, but it still felt as dark as night because she felt like something was there that she couldn't see, something evil. When she reached Diana's room door, she cracked it further open, noticing nothing odd besides the fact that her clutch and other bag that she normally carries with her when she goes out were still there, along with a few things scattered about on the floor. That was the usual Diana, not tidy at all. She went inside.

Her palm sweat with fear as she held on to the fork tighter than she'd ever held anything in her life. She looked in the closet and then she finally kneeled underneath the bed again, only to find nothing. She let out a light sigh to release tension, stood up, and went to check the locks on the window, but it was already up. Ayana stopped in her tracks but remembered that Diana was talking to them via the window, thus the reason for it being open in the first place. She immediately closed it and twisted the switch to lock, noticing that it was loose. It wasn't five minutes before there was a knock at the door.

Ayana walked to the door, wiping her eyes, in efforts to not appear as worried as she was. Before getting to the door, she stopped at the long mirror that hung at the entrance for her and Diana to check how they look before exiting. It was an old habit that Ayana picked up from her mother, to always review before giving the public a preview. That was what her mother would say, and Ayana made certain her eyes were clear of tears before opening the door.

"Hi, thanks for coming by," she stated, staring away from him and toward the sofa that sat three feet from the door. Dean noticed how she was trying to disguise her uneasiness, so he came inside, lifted her chin and comforted her.

"Things are going to be alright, okay?" He turned around to close the door behind himself, and then took her by the hand. "Let's just sit here for about fifteen more minutes, Ayana, before alerting anyone or going to look for her. I know it seems long, but the car is gone. That means that she could have just taken off somewhere real quick" he continued, but stopped when he got interrupted by her unsettled response.

"But it's already been about fifteen minutes, Dean. I can't *not* think that something's wrong. Her cell phone is even in there," she pointed towards Diana's room. "I'm getting ready to call the cops because even though it sounds like I'm being too cautious, things just don't feel right...and that's probably because they're not right. I have a bad feeling that is smothering me right now, and it's not imaginary."

"Well, look. Let's take my car and drive around the complex and further on up to the convenience stores. If we don't see her or your car, then we'll just take the situation to the University police and then, if we have to, to the county police. Alright? It hadn't even been an hour yet. Maybe someone around here saw her. If she was in danger, they maybe even heard her."

She listened to what he was saying, and it made sense. "You're right. If she was in danger, she would have thrown a fit, kicking, screaming and fighting. I would have at least heard that, shower or not. Let's just drive around, and I'll keep calling her phone. If she picks up, that means that she made it back to the house, and I can cuss her out then. Wait a second," she stated as she glanced at her vibrating cell phone. "It's my cousin." He sat down on the sofa, and then, she answered after taking a seat beside him.

"Hi, Trina."

"Hey, I thought you were supposed to call me back, girl. I know you didn't go to the party, get drunk and forget to tell me how the party went?"

"No…" she glanced up at Dean and then started talking into the phone again, deciding to cut to the chase. "No, I…I don't know where Diana is."

"What?" Trina asked with much concern in her voice.

"Diana…she came into the house, but then she just left. Took the car and went somewhere. She wasn't drinking, so she was sober. I was…"

"Where were you?" Trina cut in. "You didn't see her? Did you call her parents yet?"

"No, Trina, no. She's only been gone for like fifteen minutes tops." Ayana glanced up at Dean again. "I'm sure she will show back up. Anyway, the University police are around the corner, so if she doesn't show up…"

"Did you call her?"

Ayana almost broke down into tears because she knew the answer would send off alarm bells, causing Trina to jump into the car and head down to the campus. "Yeah, but she didn't pick up. Listen, let me call you back. I have a ride..."

"With who?"

Ayana already heard the suspicion in her cousin's voice. Trina knew her more than she knew herself, so it wasn't going to be long before Trina figured something was desperately wrong. "With someone else who I met that lives down the road. It's the same person that brought us home. She's uhm...cool." Ayana's eyes spared herself the embarrassment of having to lie by not looking Dean's way when she insinuated that he was actually a female.

"Ayana! Didn't your dad buy you a car so that you won't have to depend on anyone for a ride? You don't even know anyone up there enough to accept rides from them. I'm on the way."

"Don't tell mom and dad, and please, Trina, I'll be fine. You just got out, and I don't want you to go back," she stated, referring to the psychiatric hospital. "Just trust me. I'm a grown woman now. I'm fine. I'll keep my phone on, just in case. I'm sure she'll be back."

"What about that mace?"

Ayana had forgotten all about the mace. She had three of them. Trina was right. She should have had it on her anyway during the party, but they weren't unpacked. "I have it. I have all of them. I will call you in about an hour, okay?"

"Okay. I'll be by the phone. Love you, cousin." Trina remained on the phone until she heard Ayana speak again. She was desperate to help her cousin because deep inside her gut, she knew there was something going wrong. Unfortunately, she didn't know whether or not the feeling was real or based on her past experiences causing her to rehearse the sense of paranoia she'd lived since the deaths of her husband and child.

"I love you, too. I'll be fine. I'll call you…I promise." From there, Ayana ended the call as Dean continued to rub her back in support of what she was going through.

"My cousin is worried out of her mind now."

"I was kind of hoping that you didn't tell her just yet. People get scared before anything is even known yet. Come on," he paused to stand up from the couch in his jeans and spotless white T-shirt. "Let's go find her. She's out here. I know she is. You don't have a tracker or anything on your car?"

"Now I wish I did. Not that I know of, unless of course my dad got over intense and put one on before I left."

"I wish he did for moments like these. Let's head out."

Ayana scanned the entire area as she hurried behind Dean to his car, giving herself every opportunity to look for potential clues about Diana. Too much time had gone by for Ayana's own sense of security. As she sat in Dean's car, she gripped her phone and started to pray as she had always been taught to do, whether things were going fine or not. She needed the Lord more than ever, just like she was told she would before she left to be out on her own. She just didn't realize the chaos would begin right away. Before Dean even opened the driver's side door, her prayer was ending. It was just that fast, and it was all she needed to keep her going.

Dean sat in the car, started the engine, and Ayana's head stared straight toward Diana's bedroom window. There was absolutely no motion at or around the house besides Dean backing the car up. She could barely turn Dean's way because just the thought of having to lean on him would cause her to break down. She wasn't raised to rely on people other than her parents or the Lord for anything. This was new to her, but since her parents were an hour away, she had no choice. Dean was all she had at the moment.

"We're gonna turn over here, circle the campus, ride around by the frat houses, and on the way back, report it to the campus police. It is kind of soon, but this isn't a television show. A missing person is a missing person. There is no wait."

"Oh, I know," she said, hoping her eyes locked onto her car as they rode down the street. It was a silver Audi with a super paint job that made it appear like it came straight off the lot. It was painted last week, just one of the gifts her dad gave her for being what he considered a good child. Ayana never got in much trouble her whole entire life, making parenting an easy task for her parents. This last four years of school in college was supposed to put the icing on the cake, but school hadn't even started and the drama had already begun.

"I forgot. Your dad's a judge."

"If it's one thing I do know, it's the law."

"I hear you. Listen, Ayana, I'm sorry your night turned out like this. If she doesn't come home..."

"She will," Ayana snapped, glaring at him like he was the enemy. "She'll come back." Before she'd even realized it, she'd allowed her anxiety to explode onto him while noticing how quiet he'd gotten after her retort. "I'm sorry,

Dean. I'm just… I feel like I'm losing my mind. Forgive me." She stared back out of the window without anything else to say because all she wanted to do was find Diana.

"It's all good." He reached over and caressed her hand. "I know you're under some stress right now, and I'm here to help."

"Thanks," she stated, forcing the strength she knew she harbored to come through before the tears started to roll. "I'm praying, so I know things will be okay. They have to be." It didn't work. Tears began to form and run down her cheeks.

They drove around the entire campus, circling in and out of the parking lots, getting out of the car and walking together through spacious areas, and even checking the twenty-four hour stores that surrounded the university. There was no sign of Diana nor Ayana's car anywhere, so they had no other choice but to go to the campus police to file a missing person's report. Understandably, the officers said they would search around, but it wasn't exactly wise to call Diana missing because it hadn't even been more than two hours, no matter how out of the ordinary things seemed. It was a college campus and she was a first year college student. They told her freshmen tend to change and do things out of the ordinary once away from the watchful eyes of home. Ayana understood and walked out of the building frustrated along with Dean.

The night was still, and everything appeared warped, like Ayana was standing in the center of a vacuum tube and she had tunnel vision. At the other end of the tube was emptiness, just a line of darkness that was never ending. While she stared at the nothingness, a tap on her shoulder snapped her out of her daze.

"It's not over. She'll be back. At least he'll circle around campus to look for the car, but they're right, Ayana. It's only been an hour tops."

"Something is wrong, dammit! Something is damn wrong! I don't care what they say." Her eyes were bloodshot, and she'd started to tremble as she thought back to Diana's room that she'd left half done in order to go out and party. Everything looked ordinary to the person who knew nothing about her, but Ayana knew Diana like a book. The only thing that led Ayana to believe Diana was fine was because there wasn't a sign of a struggle, and there was one thing she knew about Diana. She would always fight if she needed to do so, no matter what. "I need to go back to the house, Dean. I just need to go back and wait."

He put his hands in the air, gesturing to her that he'd done all he could do to make her feel better. From there, he took her back to the house without argument. He appeared drained, but for her sake, willing to stick it out until Ayana's friend came back home. Despite him not wanting to come off callous or insensitive, he ended up saying something that set Ayana off in a worst way by the time they got back to what turned out to be her empty driveway.

"It was kind of early to go to the police, Ayana. I didn't want to say it, but I think you're dragging this out too much. I know we just met, and I got no real right, but did you see how she was dressed tonight at the party though?"

"Excuse me?"

"Seriously. If you just listen. She looked nice and everything, but her signals were all about one thing to a guy my age or younger. It looks like your friend may have just sneaked out to have a good time."

"Are you saying she asked for whatever has happened to her tonight? It's almost like you know what happened? Do you?" she continued, livid at that point.

"Listen to yourself, Ayana. You sound like she couldn't leave you alone without telling you everything about her whereabouts. You're in college now, and even though you're like sisters, you're not her mom. She even took the car. Don't you think there might be some things that you don't know about her even though you all have been attached all your lives? I've known people all my life as well, and I'm not even gonna lie, they don't know hardly anything about me," he said, looking her directly in her face.

Ayana jolted against the car door, staring at him with disdain and hostility, unable to say anything back. For one solid minute, the man she made out with at the side of the house and thought was one of the sexiest men she'd run into on the campus only looked like a prick with an attitude instead of a friend, much less a boyfriend.

"Leave me the fuck alone. Thanks for everything, but stay the hell away from me," she stated under her breath as she snatched her arm away from him. He tried to keep her from leaving the car in such a rage but failed. When he felt her pull away from his arm, he hopped out of the car and met her in front of the car.

"Listen, Ayana, I know we just met, but…"

"But you think I'm a damn fool? Man, Dean, my friend is missing," she stressed while pointing at the empty spot in the driveway where her car was once parked. "She doesn't just take off with my car like that, and she never leaves her phone, much less a full plate of food. This late at night, Dean? Really? Keep being ignorant because I'm not. Why should you care?"

"You shouldn't go back in there alone. You're just not thinking clearly, Ayana. Come on back to my place."

"I'm calling my father, and you should leave. I'll be fine."

"Ayana," he called, but it was too late. She entered the house, leaving him alone on the cobblestone that led to her front door. As soon as she shut the door, she locked it and flicked on the light. The place was just as empty as when she left, but she became startled by a ringing noise from outside her door. She peaked out of the peephole and noticed Dean picking up his phone. Just then, her phone rang as well. It was Trina.

"I'm on the way. I've been driving for at least forty minutes, Ayana. I had a bad feeling," Trina said. "This whole thing doesn't make sense to me because I know you two like old, rundown books. You're not being straight with me."

"You can't come down here, Trina. You just got out. They'll send you back if something goes wrong. Just go back home. I'm fine, and I'm in the house," Ayana pleaded, believing that her parents would unravel.

"How on the earth will those people back at the ward know where I went?" There was a silence. "I thought so. And I didn't tell your parents. The only person who knows where I am is you, so don't act stupid on me Ayana. I'm coming up. I know how this works. Someone sees you at a party and then," she paused, "It's the same thing that happened to me except mine found me in a grocery store, some maniac."

"I'm not you!" Ayana screamed, tired of her cousin checking on her like she was still a child.

"And you don't have to be me! That's exactly the point! I don't want what happened to me to happen to you!" Trina screamed back. "I'm not exactly crazy. I lost everything I ever had, but I'm not crazy. There's a big difference, Ayana. A big difference. Don't play me like that because the same thing could happen to you, and that's why I'm coming."

"And if you're wrong, Trina?"

"Better safe than committed to an asylum or the grave. I already know where you live. I sneaked the address from your mom's book. Bye."

The call ended and Ayana stormed down the hallway, dropped onto her bed, and cried. "Everything's going wrong, just wrong! Diana, where are you? Where are you?" she asked in a pitiful moan. The first weekend at the school was turning into a nightmare. Even if Ayana had to go somewhere, she couldn't because the car was gone which placed her at odds within the house, so much so that she started to kick and throw things all over the room. There was no stopping her hopelessness as she stood in the middle of her four white walls. Everything in her life that she thought was secure began unraveling all because of the haunting hunch that something had happened to Diana.

She finally pulled herself together, beginning to think about everyone she saw at the party. She tried to recall every face that they passed by on the way to the party, to whom they smiled and spoke. She remembered locking the front door specifically. The knob turned and stopped right afterward. She even jiggled it. The door was locked.

Then, she thought about how she entered the house after she and Dean parted ways. Even then, she made certain she locked the door, but she paused in mid-thought. She never really heard Diana inside. She only assumed that she was in the bedroom, but was she?

Immediately, she second guessed her original account of Diana even being in the room from the very beginning. Following her instinct, she walked out of her room and into the hallway. In mid-step, she paused. There was a noise from inside Diana's room. The noise was very distinct, like something falling up against the side of a drawer or bed rail. With the phone held steadily in the palm of her hand, she nervously dialed Diana's phone. She reached behind herself and planted her body against the wall, not for certain what was coming next. The sounds…they really didn't sound like the typical Diana. Besides that, she'd already locked the window, and no one came in the door behind her.

As Ayana glanced at the front door from her silent stance in the hallway, Diana's phone rang once. An agonizing chill ran down her spine as she listened, hoping the phone would be answered. Her left hand held on to the ridges of the doorway as the second ring started, but before it finished, the cell phone was answered. Ayana's face lit up as her body released all the tension and her fingers let go of the wall. She burst through Diana's bedroom door.

"Diana, girl, where have you been?" The words escaped her mouth before her brain caught up with what she actually saw - a man standing in front of her. He held something inside his right hand, and in the other hand, he held Diana's cell phone.

"He dropped his school ID," he stated with a smile that cocked to the side of his face. He watched Ayana fall back into the doorway with her mouth gaped open, her words trapped somewhere in between him and her throat. He then continued talking, shrugging his shoulders, indifferent to her fears, "This used to be my room."

117

Ayana recalled the identification card that was on the floor of Diana's room when she scanned it. She didn't turn it over because she didn't believe it was anything out of the ordinary, but when she zoomed in on the identification that dangled from Dean's fingertips, she bolted from the room, screaming for help. It wasn't Diana's identification card. It belonged to someone else.

Her body pounded against the wall as she lost her footing, but when she spotted Dean right behind her, she forcefully pushed herself forward. She then swung her arm around to hit him in the face because he was just that close to her, but when she did, her efforts to get away became impeded by his strength.

"Where you going, Ayana, huh? Where you going?" Dean clamped down on her hair with the agility of an angry animal in the wild, catching her without much effort, yanking her backwards. She landed hard against his chest, but she didn't stop her fight to get away.

"Help me!" she screamed her loudest and hardest for anyone to come from anywhere, but he covered her mouth, picked her entire body up from the floor, and threw her back down. Pain ripped through Ayana's arm and shoulder when the side of her body was launched to the floor, but she continued to claw the carpet until he straddled her body, flipped her over like a ragdoll, and placed his hand around her throat. Although she could still breathe, the shock of the situation caused her to stop breathing in horror as she thought he would eventually lock onto her neck harder and ultimately kill her.

The throb of Ayana's heart sped up until she lost all her power, having been overcome with dread as Dean's disturbing stare rushed into the innermost parts of her being, rendering her incapable of escaping or fighting back. She felt her pulse thumping beyond the vessels of her neck while confusion finally became overcome with answers - that it had been Dean all along, and he wasn't working alone.

"This was my old spot when I was a sophomore. I saw you, Ayana," he laughed. "I saw you. Look." His eyes moved across the walls and even on the ceiling before looking back down at her. "Even when you called me," he continued, leaning down to her ear and whispering, "I saw you. I told you I would know it was you."

"Get off of me!" Ayana screamed terrified of who was now an unknown man on top of her. Terror rose inside Ayana like steam from a boiling pot of water, choking her worse than his hands that were around her throat. Her eyes moved to every single space in the house where she could get a visual. He'd been watching her the whole time, ever since they'd moved in. Tears began to flow from her eyes as she felt the shame of him knowing her every move. Finally, she swung her hardest at his face, but missed. Dean found it humorous. He then grabbed her swinging arms and slammed them to the ground.

"Nobody can hear you. Absolutely no one can hear you, Ayana. It's just me and you, baby girl. Just me and you…and now we have to go." He let her arms loose and a horror stricken Ayana was afraid to move them another inch. "Get up. When you get up, be quiet." He spoke with a smile, but she knew it was because he was out of his mind. Therefore, she listened.

She slowly lifted her finger to her own trembling mouth, signaling to Dean that she will quiet down on her own and do whatever it was that he wanted her to do. Nodding her head, she begged him with her eyes to not hurt her. He even took her by the hand and lifted her from the floor. Ayana disguised her terror as much as she could as her eyes

119

became disciple to his hand, following it as it led her to the bedroom window that he came through. Then, he let her hand go in order to kneel down and lock both his hands around her ankles. At that point, any idea she had of yelling or leaping disappeared, leaving her escape from reality going shut with the window as it glided down with her hands. She then locked it shut. His hands loosened their grips on her ankles, and then he stood tall in front of her, admiring what he saw. Ayana glanced at the bed, in an attempt to stall because she knew her cousin was on the way there. All she needed to do was remain inside the house, but when he noticed her shift toward the bed, he stopped her.

"I have a girlfriend for that, Ayana," he stated, shrugging his shoulders confidently. "What? I'm sorry that you fell for that shit back there I told you. You hollered at me first, remember? I just answered," he continued, dragging his finger up her stomach as she yanked her body back. "Maybe not how you wanted me to answer, but I answered, sweetheart." He motioned his eyes toward the door and took Ayana by the hand. "For now, let's just walk." He tightened his grip around her fingers so much so that it hurt and warned her dementedly, "Don't try shit. Nothing. Just out the door and to my car." He smiled again. "Just like you held me before. You don't want me to end up being seen going out the window the same way I came inside, do you? By the way, baby girl, that window never locks…for me anyway."

Ayana walked with him to the front door, calming herself down in a hope to keep herself alive long enough for someone to find her and Diana. She wasn't sure what was going to happen to her, but she decided to take it one step at a time.

There was a long blade that he pulled from the back of his pants, and he moved it toward her shirt. Ayana's body caved as the knife came toward her. She shook her head violently, and his other hand quickly shut her mouth as he placed the knife underneath her shirt and stood directly behind her. Ayana's breathing became erratic and a swarm of tears followed as she imagined her lifeless body dropping to the floor, struggling to remain alive.

"Now, we're going to walk out of here close to one another, just like we did earlier," he explained as he kissed her on her neck, relishing with the way her body cringed. "Hide my knife for me under your shirt, okay, baby?" he asked as he positioned his body directly against hers like they were in a lovers' caressing hug, all this while his left hand never left from underneath her shirt, holding the knife in place. He reached for the door knob, but before he turned it, there was a knock on the door. His eyes shot forward and the knife cut her skin. When she jerked, he shoved his hand over her mouth and whispered in her ear. "Don't move. Don't you fucking move or say a word." His breathing became heavy, and sweat began to bubble up on his neck and forehead, however, he didn't wipe as the second set of knocks to the door came. His head was directly in front of the peephole, and he could see straight out of it. It was obvious to Ayana why he wasn't moving. Everyone knew that if the light from the peephole changed, someone was on the other side.

"Ms. Ayana Tate? This is the University police. We wanted to look around in your home a bit after we had a report of a possible kidnapping. Are you at home?" He said with another knock at the door. "Ms. Ayana Tate?"

Each time the officer called her by name, she cried. The tears ran down her cheeks, but Dean didn't let up. She didn't want that to be the very last time she heard her name ever called. As the force of Dean's hand across her mouth worsened, she heard the officer move away from the door, and her heart dropped as Dean's slanted his eyes down at her. Before he could speak, Ayana's phone rang. It echoed through the house and caused Dean to panic. He looked out the peephole, and his heart dropped at what he saw, resulting in him snatching the knife out from underneath Ayana's shirt only to shove her back down the hallway, him following behind. He shoved her once again after she picked the cell phone off of the hallway floor, forcing her into her bedroom.

"Answer the damn phone, and if you talk too much, your friend is dead," he explained as he gripped his cell phone in his hand. "Now, pick that shit up nice, easy, and breathe like he just woke you up. Make him leave."

"Hello," Ayana spoke into the receiver as she shrank in fear in front of Dean who stood before her with a knife to her temple. He was visibly bothered, blinking erratically, and looking all around the room and then back at her. He was losing his mind.

"Ms. Tate, this is Officer Melbourne at your front door. I knocked a couple times. Since you came by about your roommate, I decided to come look around inside after searching this area. Are you inside?"

The question threw Ayana off guard, and she didn't know what to say off the top of her head because her natural instinct wanted to take over and scream for help. However, the knife directly at her head and the life of her lost friend that she wanted to save kept her thoughts together as she answered the officer.

"Well, I was lying down, officer, with some company, but I can get up if you give me a second to change..." she stuttered, "and my man some time to get some clothes on, too, I can..."

"Take your time. I'll be out...better yet...I'll just," he continued, but Ayana sensed he was getting ready to leave which was something that she didn't want. She wanted the officer to get a look at Dean, a good look at him, so that he would know that Dean was the last person with her.

"No, no, it's fine, officer, we'll get dressed again, and you can take a look. Just a minute. " She then glanced up into Dean's eyes which were no longer loving but full of hatred and despair. She knew that if something went wrong, she would die. She ended the call, placing the cell phone directly on her bed.

"Put on a robe."

Ayana rushed to her closet and yanked down a thick robe, however, when she was draping it across her body, he grabbed her, shoving her into the bathroom. "Look at your face."

Ayana's hands held on to the sink like it was the last thing she would ever touch and lifted her head to see herself in the mirror. He shoved her head closer to it, and then spoke crushing her neck so hard that she thought it would pop. Then, he suddenly let go.

"Act like you love me because if I get caught, I got nothing to lose. I'll fucking kill you right here in front of him. When you let him in, you will walk with me, your hand in mine." Then, she watched as he slid the knife into his pants pocket, dropping his shirt over it in order to conceal. "It's just as close to you as I am. He won't be able to shoot me fast enough, sweetheart."

She listened as she focused on each part of his face through the mirror. Ayana was terrified, not because he had the knife, but because he was right. Cop or no cop, she knew that regardless, he could hurt or even kill her, and the police wouldn't be able to do a thing because there was no way he would be on time to save her life. Therefore, she responded in direct obedience formed from sheer terror.

"Okay," she whispered, taking a deep breath to calm herself. "I understand." Then, she willingly took his hand so that he saw her effort, and that made him smile considering that he had total control of the situation. They proceeded to the front door, hand in hand, as her hand went numb at the thought of cradling his.

When she got to the front door, it was Dean who decided to open it and greet the officer. "Officer?"

The officer turned back to face the door as Dean extended his left hand for a handshake. Ayana watched, and everything felt like it was going in slow motion, quite opposite the panic that was moving through her veins starting at the connection of her flesh with Dean's flesh.

"I'm sorry to bother you all. It'll be just a minute," he stated, glancing at Ayana who remained silent. "I just need to," he continued as Dean stepped away, hinting to Ayana to move away from the door by squeezing her hand, "come inside and look around after a report that came through of a possible kidnapping in the area right after you two left the office."

"What about a kidnapping?" Dean asked as he watched the officer step inside. He noticed that the officer was relaxed for the most part, almost as if he'd planned on not finding anything versus locating any clues on Diana's disappearance.

"Somebody anonymously called in and said they saw a male and female walking from this way. They didn't see what happened clearly because they were driving by but said that it appeared like someone was put in the trunk of a car. It's your car that's missing, right?"

"Yes...yes sir. It's my car. Did they say what the car looked like? Diana, she's Puerto Rican, and she...my car..." Ayana stammered, but Dean squeezed her hand tighter and brought her in closer to him, rubbing her back and placing her head onto his chest.

"It's alright. Let him look around. She's not doing too good. All she's been doing is just what you heard, rambling...and I was about to get her mind off some things before the phone call," Dean smirked. The officer then turned toward Ayana and proceeded to the back rooms.

"Which room is hers?"

"It's the one on the right," Ayana responded with a hint of fear and desperation in her voice that caused Dean to place his hand on his knife while he watched the officer walk back into the room, ignoring what he considered a cocky comment from the young man standing before him.

"Officer, we're gonna sit right here while you check around. Ayana's getting upset all over again, so we'll be out here. Feel free." He looked down at the top of Ayana's head. "Come on over here with me and calm down. Everything's gonna be fine..." Then his tone deepened and decreased to a whisper. "It better be."

Time didn't fly. The full minute the officer was inside Diana's room felt like thirty. As stoic as Ayana sat on the couch, she thought that the officer would notice how tense she was once he'd gotten out of the room. However, when he came back into the living area, he didn't notice anything unusual, on her or in the room.

"Thank you. I'll go ahead and get out of here, but you let me know if you hear or see anything suspicious. In the meantime, we'll go ahead and put out your car as stolen, and unfortunately, we'll have to contact your friend's family due to the phone call we received, just to be on the safe and proper side of things. We have the information at the station, correct?"

"Yes…and, officer," she called, standing up, however, not able to remove herself from Dean's grip. "Please," she stated, staring him directly in his eyes as tears dripped from hers. "Help me…" There was a slight pause, and as she hesitated, her heart thumping harder than a drummer on a drumline, Dean stood up behind her. The thought of him stabbing her with the knife became overwhelming, and she finally continued, "Help me find her. She's my best friend." She appeared mortified as she stood there, and the officer examined her for a brief second, looked at Dean and then back at Ayana.

"Take care of her. Let her get some rest. Things will be fine. We'll handle things down at the station, and it's up to you if you want to call and tell her parents first. Personally, I think you should go ahead and do so before we do…all in good taste being that it was you who filed the report. We are treating this as a missing person's case. We have your statements, so goodnight until sun up." As he walked out, he finalized his visit. "If anything changes, please call us."

"Thank you, officer." Ayana frightfully watched the door close behind him. She just stood there. Everything else was nonexistent besides herself and the departing officer. An insatiable craving to escape filled her veins. She wanted to scream, but couldn't. It was too late.

"Shh, baby girl," he stated quietly as he listened for the squad car door to slam while he walked in front of her. His eyes destroyed any ounce of hope that she had of getting away while he emptied hatred onto her with his morbid stare. Ayana couldn't hold her tears back any longer as he enjoyed terrorizing her with his presence. Finally, he looked away from her, and when he did, Ayana found her chance to run. She bolted directly toward her bedroom without looking back. It wasn't five seconds before she slammed the bedroom door shut that she heard him on the other side of the door.

Ayana's entire body quaked at the sound of his giggle, causing her to squeeze the lock even harder, terrified of him gaining entry. Her palms began sweating on the small lock as she twisted around in search of anything to help her protect herself. There was nothing, so she dove to the window. Before she even got it unlocked, the crash at the bedroom door made things even more real as she struggled to push the window up.

"Help me!" Her hands pounded the window until her face slammed against the glass and her body was thrown down to the floor. "Get off of me! Help me, please!" she screamed, kicking herself backwards toward the broken bedroom door. Everywhere she moved was a trap, and even when she looked upward at him hovering over her like a madman, she knew he was too strong to defeat.

Each time she kicked, Dean swiped her legs, causing her to lose balance, slow down and connect with the floor in a brutal way. "Where you going?" he shouted. "Answer me!"

"Leave me alone!" She kicked in his direction again, finally connecting with his kneecap. He buckled as she launched more kicks his way, but her kicks were halted as soon as she reached the doorway of the bedroom. He'd regained his footing and dragged her back into the bedroom.

She watched herself grow centimeters and then inches away from her bedroom door. Ayana had finally stopped begging, wailing and crying for mercy. There was only one thing she wanted to do with her strength and that was fight for her life. She flipped herself over to sit up and strike him with her fist, landing her target. Then, with her other hand, she went for his face again, still struggling to set her legs free from his grip. One of his hands fell, and that was when she struck his face again. Then he reached in the side of this pants, retrieving the knife that she'd already been cut with on her stomach. Before she could even counter his swing, it was all over. She died there on the bedroom floor. He'd stabbed her twice, the second wound proving fatal as she struggled to breathe from the gash in her neck.

He allowed her leg to fall, watching her blood run out onto the floor. The last place her pupils met were his, and that was when he knew, he'd messed up. His hands covered his face while he turned himself around in a full circle, but when he took them down, he started to dial on his phone, placing the knife on the dresser. "Shit…" he stated, as he picked it back up while answering another person on the line. "I lost it, Rick. Rick, man, there's blood. A cop came by, she hit me, man, and…" As he was talking, he heard a knock at the door. He snatched the phone from his ear, and listened again. There it was again, another knock that caused him to fold. Lifting the phone back to his ear, he sprang into action, dragging Ayana's body to the side of the wall. "Shit, Rick, somebody's here!"

**

"Dean, man what the hell? Blood, man? I asked you to get the ID. What the hell happened?" Rick shouted into the phone and he flashed an irritated look at Diana who sat on a couch with one of her ankles tied to its leg. She sensed trouble, but had no idea it had to do with Ayana. "Man, damn. Talk! I told you to lay low and just get my damn ID. What the fuck, man?" Rick's eyes turned bloodshot, and it was plain as the night's moon that he knew things had gone wrong. "Come on, man, tell me something. You didn't kill her..."

"Help me, somebody!" Diana cried, but that prompted the light toned, biracial Rick to walk over to her and slap her face so hard that she became dizzy, slumping over in the chair. Then he turned his attention back to the phone, satisfied with the daze he'd put Diana into.

"Now tell me, Dean," he whispered, "Is she dead?"

"Yeah, yeah... she is, and I gotta go. I need a way outta here without being seen, Rick," Dean whispered on the other line, listening closely as he heard the front door open. Quickly, he thought about when the police left the house. No one locked the door. "Man, shit, I need a way out." He glanced at the window. "That damn window is sealed shut, man."

"Well, get the hell outta there, man. We'll go to the dungeon for this, man. What the hell?" Rick continued, glancing quickly around the shack like he was looking for something to calm him down. Then, his eyes fell back on a dazed Diana, and he took a deep breath before speaking again. "This is all fucked up. Make sure she's dead, Dean, and then meet me back here." He ended the call just that fast and tucked his phone into his pants pocket, having already decided to abandon the shack and leave Dean all on his own. He walked over to Diana and untied her ankle from the couch. Then, he quickly released her wrist from the pole that was located beside the arm of the couch. "You're free to go, doll. Here are the keys." He wiped them off good although he had on gloves the whole time he was with her, and then he tossed the keys onto the couch.

Diana didn't know what to do, so she just sat there pretending to be light headed from the slap the masked man gave her. She turned slowly and faced the keys, afraid to budge one inch while allowing what she heard him say digest in her gut. He said Dean. The guy that gave them a ride back to the house, bought them breakfast…and the same one that she called out for earlier that day from the window. Diana held back her tears as she watched the man who took her against her will scramble out of the house, and once he left, she fell to the floor crying.

"Ayana!" she cried, "Please, please don't be dead!" The words her kidnapper stated replayed over and over in her head. Suddenly, she remembered what was about to happen and soon. Her kidnapper told Dean to meet him where she was located. "Oh God," she cried, ripping the set of keys from the couch while realizing that her kidnapper was ditching his partner. She'd been blindfolded all the way up to the time she was roped to the couch, so she had no idea where she was when she ran through the door.

Stumbling to a stop as she exited, she was stunned to watch the back of a car speeding off from the rundown house. From the corner of her eye, she watched as the tail lights from the car became dim in the foggy distance. Afraid to follow him, she turned around in circles until she saw where Ayana's car was located and ran toward it. The alarm sounded from her pressing the panic button to get anyone's attention, and as she jumped into the automobile, she locked the doors and screamed. The wail was so tremendous that her neck throbbed as she leaned her head on the steering wheel. She didn't understand any of what just happened to her, but she needed to find her way home.

Diana lifted her bruised face from the steering wheel and searched beyond the fog as far as she could. Keeping the lights off, in terror, she started to drive slowly until she stopped the car. Tension started to rise and create pain in her shoulders as she trembled, raising her eyes to stare in the back seat. She thought she was all alone, but felt like someone was still watching her closely. She lifted her eyes slowly as her body completely caved to the paranoia that overtook her soul, and as she peered weakly through the rear view mirror, she swung her arm backward and released a horrible shriek. Diana didn't stop swinging until she turned fully to only discover that she was truly alone in the car. There was just a teddy bear, Ayana's brown teddy bear, sitting in the backseat as usual, staring back at her. Her mind, then, went straight back to her closest friend in the world – Ayana. She spun the car around, wiped her eyes, and began to search her way out of a part of town she knew nothing about, and she dared not stop.

**

"Ayana?" Trina opened the door. "Ayana, it's me, Trina," she called as she allowed the door to swing backwards against the wall. She received no answer. "Ayana!" she called even louder. Ayana's not answering was all Trina needed to let her know that something was wrong. From the small, double stepped porch, she scanned the front room. "Ayana, you left your door open, sweetheart!" She reached down to her side, but realized that she jumped from the car, leaving her purse. Quickly, she turned around wanting to run back to the side of the house and grab it in order to retrieve her cell phone, however, when she took a step back, there was a sound that echoed from the back room. "Ayana?" From there, Trina stepped inside.

The house was quiet, with the feeling of someone just stepping out for a moment. Again, Trina looked behind herself. There was no one outside. From there, she walked to the kitchen, which was to her left in the living room dining room combo, to find the first thing to defend herself. Keeping her eyes on the hallway, she fumbled through the drawers as silently as she could, but found nothing. Frustrated but very alert, she pulled the whole drawer out, emptied it, and decided that would be her weapon if need be.

There was still no one at or coming through the front door that she left wide open, and the nighttime air blew inside, almost calming to the fretful undercurrent. The streets were empty and the neighbors were too far spaced out to hear anything vitally important, including her continuous calls for Ayana.

"Ayana! Are you here? Baby cousin," she called as she walked toward the hallway. There was a small glass on the counter that she picked up on the way. She tossed it to the back of the hall and watched as it hit the wall and fall to the floor. Nothing happened after that. She noticed absolutely no movement, so she made her way back, a bit faster than her original gait inside the house.

Not knowing which room belonged to Ayana, she stopped at the first room to her right – Diana's room. She crept inside whispering, "Ayana? It's me Trina." The room wasn't exactly clean, but nothing triggered a worse vibe than what Trina already had besides the cold food that sat on the bed. She walked a little further inside, but when she saw no sign of Ayana she backed up, holding the kitchen drawer firmly in front of her chest. She readjusted her fingers and turned around slowly, gathering everything she saw mentally…until she felt the presence of a physical being standing right behind her. Without hesitation, she looked up but was shoved backwards by a knife that went straight through the thin wood of the kitchen drawer.

Trina screamed and thrusted the drawer toward the assailant as he lunged at her once again while breaking the drawer away from his knife. Trina immediately rubbed her hand all over her shirt in horror believing she'd been stabbed due to the force of the drawer that was propelled against her chest. Everything on Diana's dresser got hauled toward the intruder as Trina tried to save her own life. She turned to grab the window and it lifted open without much effort. She jumped head first from the window, but was dragged back inside as she fought to hold on to the outside brick. The man was too strong. He delivered what felt like a large punch to her back that forced the wind from her body, and then he flipped her over, half of her body hanging out of the window. Then, she watched the knife come down and enter her abdomen three times before going limp. Raising her eyes, she saw him staring back at her with a straight face, like he'd done nothing wrong. As he pulled her entire body back inside the window, Trina's eyes fell shut.

**

"Come on," Diana mumbled as she raced the car down the interstate. She ended up locating the highway that would take her directly to the university, and she hopped on it. It didn't feel like that was the route taken when she was placed in the car, but it was the only way she knew to find her way back to her campus home. "Come on!" she finally yelled, feeling like the car was driving slower than the weight of the foot on the gas pedal. "Go!" She didn't care if she was pulled over in the car because in her mind, she wanted the cops coming behind her anyway. All she could think about was the safety of Ayana, and due to the fact that she got out alive, she was praying constantly down the road that what she overheard her kidnapper saying was a total lie. There was no way she could call the police or the ambulance to get there before she did. Her only option was to get there for her best friend, the closest friend she'd ever had in all of her life.

The next exit was the exit that she would get off on, so she quickly made a right, nearly throwing the car off the road and into a ditch, pressing on the gas even harder. The roads were silent, a few cars here and there, but mainly Diana was on her own. Although she scanned the roads in search of a police officer, she found not one. Beeping the horn as much as she could didn't help garner attention either, so she flipped on the emergency lights as she sped down the familiar road toward the university. Soon, she was able to see her house from the road, and she jumped the sidewalk in order to speed directly to front door. The front door was wide open, but regardless of her fears, Diana jumped out of the running car and headed towards the porch on foot.

"Ayana!" she cried loudly, her hands twisted in her hair. She squeezed her head tightly as the tears rolled down her face. "Ayana!" Diana spun around on the small porch and called out as loudly as she could, "Somebody help us! Help us, please!" Then, she ran back down to her car and laid her entire palm on the horn for one minute to alert anyone down the road. She stopped when she saw a light come on down the road, and yelled once again for help.

Finally, she bolted back up the porch and into the house all alone.

As soon as her feet hit the floor, there was more rage overtaking her than fear. "I'm gonna kill your ass if you hurt Ayana! You hear me? I'm talking to you, Dean! I know who you are, you stupid, ugly mother fucker! I'm gonna kill you!" While she spoke she ran toward the kitchen and noticed one of the drawers was removed. She looked for something to use to defend herself but found nothing, so she prepared herself to fight with her own strength.

She walked firmly down the hallway, ready to fight with all she had, but when her attention escaped her and directed itself onto her bedroom, she fell against the wall and screamed. "Ayana!" Diana's heart plummeted to her feet as she broke free from her trance and darted toward what appeared to be her friend's dead body. When she got to the body, she knew immediately that it wasn't Ayana. Upon turning the limp body over, Trina was revealed, and Diana clasped her hands on the sides of Trina's head, elevating it in order to find some life left within her. "Trina, don't be dead, Trina!" Trina's eyes moved slightly, and Diana screamed in a fit of joy. "Trina, I'm turning you over on your side and calling the ambulance. Stay with me, please. Who did this? Was it Dean? Trina!"

Diana began to search Trina's pockets for a phone but she didn't find it. Then, she looked for her own phone, but couldn't find it anywhere in the room. "God!" she screamed, panicking while Trina laid dying on the floor. She ran out of the room and into Ayana's, but when she entered, she fell to her knees at the sight of Ayana's body draining blood from her stomach and neck. Just by the sight of her once beautiful brown skin changing into a morbid color, she knew her friend was dead.

"Oh God,"she crawled over to her, almost afraid to move her in any way. "I'm sorry, Ayana," she wept horribly, unable to stop trembling in the agony of the moment. "I'm so sorry," she continued to cry over and over again. "I didn't know Dean was the other man...I heard on the phone," she struggled to explain herself to a deceased Ayana. "If I would have known, I would have fought while you were in the bathroom, but I didn't know. I thought I was protecting you," she sobbed. "I thought I was protecting you!" she finally screamed. Diana, after her thoughts raced back to Trina, reached over Ayana's lifeless body and shut her eyelids. "I love you, Ayana." She'd already spotted Ayana's phone, so she took it from the bed and dialed.

"Hello? I need help." She bursted into tears. "Send an ambulance fast, please. My family is dead...they're dead," she moaned, collapsing onto the edge of the bed. "Dean killed them. I know he did it. Send the police, please..." she stated, first calmly and then erupted, "Hurry up, they're dying!" Her emotions became volatile, and it was obvious that she could no longer control them. She ripped the sheet down from the bed, and carefully placed it atop Ayana, said a prayer in her native tongue, and left her inside the room.

Her feet felt like lead as she exited Ayana's bedroom, feeling overtaken by loss, guilt and trouble accepting the fact that she was walking away from her only true friend. She also knew that she had to care for Trina in the best way that she possibly could until help arrived. Therefore, she went to sit by Trina's side until she heard the sirens come. The dispatch operator was still on the telephone, but Diana wasn't talking. She stared straight ahead while cradling Trina's head, rubbing her cheeks with soft strokes until she was moved away from her by the arriving paramedics.

It wasn't long before the police questioned Diana with her parents by her side. Ayana and Trina's parents arrived at the hospital, their hearts broken and yet hopeful for Trina who received a prognosis of almost certain survival. During the process of Diana divulging as much information about her kidnapping as she could to law enforcement, it was discovered that there was no person named Dean documented that lived in the area that was enrolled at the university. Despite the university identification that was shown to them after the party, there was no Dean fitting the description or license tag that she'd memorized. It belonged to an old woman who lived only three blocks away from their home, thus, the tags were stolen. Unfortunately, the officers believed that the suspect Dean did possibly live there before, but off record, as a friend to someone else. Diana never heard the name of the person who put her in the trunk of the car nor could she describe him. All she could tell them was that he took her to a place, and she couldn't take them back to that place if she tried. The whole case left the detectives with hardly any clues besides the vacant home down the road where they found a small recording of the inside of Ayana's home to go along with the hidden cameras in the walls of their house. The case went unsolved although there were countless sketches and postings of the Dean that killed Ayana.

Two Years Later

"I'm getting ready to hop in the shower, Trina! I'm totally stink from my workout. I'll be out in a second," Diana called from the bathroom. She'd gotten on with her life fairly well with Trina by her side. Diana was there each and every moment as Trina's wounds healed, and Trina didn't even have to return to the psychiatric hospital. Having to speak at Ayana's funeral was the hardest thing Diana had to do, however, she pushed herself through it, and in the end, received a blessing from Ayana's parents. Since it was both Ayana's and Diana's dream of finishing college, Ayana's father paid for her enrollment into another university six months after the death of his daughter while Trina enrolled at a nearby technical college to brush up on advanced business skills to open her own business finally. Trina's parents gifted one year's rent paid as long as her grades remained up and she continued to progress from the torments of her life. The young ladies were determined to not allow evil to destroy the good that they could bring to their lives and the world, remembering that Ayana would have wanted it that way.

"Alright. I'm out here looking up different designs for my logo, trying to get some ideas," she replied, then began talking to herself. "This logo thing is really ridiculous," she stated, moaning through a deep breath of frustration.

There was a framed picture of her baby on the coffee table, and she would always look at it to remind herself to keep going. She glanced at it and smiled, "I'm doing it, sweetheart. Mama's doing it…" That was when the idea hit her – to make a logo from her baby's features. She stood up full of joy, picked up the frame and laid a huge kiss on her child's photo. "Thank you! Oh, how I love you…and your daddy…" Just then, there was a knock at the door. She peeped through the peephole.

"Who is it?"

"I'm the apartment exterminator. Do I need to come back at another time, ma'am? I just need to walk through and spray. Take five minutes."

"Oh sure," Trina replied, having already given him the glance over through the peephole. He wore a regular uniform with a tag hanging off the pocket, a cap along with the exterminator equipment in his hand. She opened the door, and there he stood. Trina had no worries. "Come on inside. Help yourself to the little monsters. Will I be in your way sitting here? Do I need to not breathe…"

"No ma'am. Go on about your normal routine. I wear this over my nose because I've gotten sensitive to it being around the chemicals all day." From there, the exterminator sprayed through the kitchen, the outdoor patio and the living area, and just like he said, he was only there for a couple minutes. "Have a good day, ma'am."

"Thank you, and you do the same." The door shut and Trina went to lock it back immediately, however, when she turned the lock, there was another knock. She didn't look out the peephole, assuming it was the exterminator again…and she was right.

"Ma'am, may I use your telephone please. My charge just died and I have to call in before my next stop to another complex. I would appreciate it. It'll be really fast."

Trina smiled, canvassed the area around him quickly with her eyes and then responded, "Sure, let me get it for you. Hold on." She'd left her cell phone on the side table next to the sofa. As she passed her child's picture, she smiled again, reached over the arm of the chair and then turned around. There he stood, his cloth nose guard off, completely inside the apartment with the door closed. Trina glanced down at the knob. The door was locked.

Trina stood in place as her eyes remained focused on the locked door, and then her body started to feel flushed with fear as she looked back at him. He wasn't the exterminator. She'd forgotten what he looked like during the attack that left her with stab wounds in her abdomen and struggling to live. Trina wasn't even able to give a good description of the Dean that Diana was able to describe so perfectly. However, she knew it was him...and he was coming straight for her.

In only two steps, he was directly in front of her. Trina called Diana, but it was too late. He lifted her by her neck, covered her mouth and nose, and waited. Trina dropped her cell phone, and as the tears ran down her face, her head finally dropped as he plastered her body against the wall. Then, he smiled, and turned his attention toward the bathroom where he heard water running.

It was these two women who were the only ones who could identify him, and without them, he would never be caught. Upon any arrest for any misdemeanor, the cops would have the opportunity to match him up with the sketch, but without his identifiers, he was free. He'd become a master at emulation and identity thefts, and he knew that the only thing standing in the way of his permanent freedom was Diana.

Everything was quiet. Diana stepped out of the shower and wiped the bathroom mirror clear of the fresh steam that moisturized the dry air. She wrapped the towel around her body, and then brushed her hair up into a ponytail. Since the death of Ayana, she refused to cut her hair. It was always a joke that one day they would both cut their long hair, make it into a wig and trade. There were lots of things that Diana couldn't let go of, and making a wig of her hair for Ayana was one of them. Before she stepped out of the bedroom, her phone rang.

"Hello?" she answered, as she wiped the mist from her phone. "Hold on, ma, let me go to my room."

"You're in the shower, aren't you?" her mother asked on speaker. "I feel like I'm on the top of a mountain or in a cave with the loud echo."

"Stop complaining, ma," she laughed. "Happy Mother's Day. I love you."

"You take that phone everywhere."

"I know, ma. Habit is all," she said, opening the bathroom door. "What time are you getting home so I can meet you there?" Diana asked as she skipped into her room, pushing the bedroom door so lightly that it didn't shut. The sun shone straight through the sheer white curtains, and she allowed the heat to massage her moist skin.

"I'm pulling in now actually, so you can come on over. I can't wait to sit back and watch my children cook for me for a change."

Diana dropped her head in a smile and giggled, "Ha, ha, mom. We cook for you all the time."

"Yeah, restaurant style and the main ingredient is dinero," her mom sarcastically stated. "Is Trina coming down as well? Surely her parents want to see her, too."

"Actually, yeah, but let me make sure." She opened her eyes and lifted her head from enjoying the feeling of the sun against her hair and arms and called, "Trina! Trina! Are you still coming?" She got no answer. "Hold on, ma." She tossed the phone on the bed and turned around, when a knife slid deeply across her throat. Her body dropped to the floor, landing on her knees, and she clasped her neck while staring back into the eyes of Dean.

"No! Dean! Help me!" Diana screamed waking up from nearly drowning in the tub full of warm water she'd run for herself after her workout. The water splashed upwards and all over the bathroom floor as her hands beat the water believing that it was Dean standing over her with a bloody knife. "Trina!" She called as she stepped out of the tub, shaken immensely by the nightmare that nearly took her life.

As she wrapped the towel around her body quickly, she leaned over to let the water flow down the drain. Then, she sat on the edge of the tub and began to wipe the creeping tears off of her face which eventually transformed into nervous laughter. She then stood up and walked to the mirror, and her neck was the first place she looked. "All together," she whispered. "Yep, it was just a bad dream." Her phone rang. "Hello?" She picked up the brush and put her hair in a quick ponytail. It was Trina on the other end.

"Diana, I just wanted to let you know that I forgot all about a meeting I had with my class group, you know for that business class I'm taking, and I'm freaking late. I just left. I don't know how long I'm going to be because this is like a big assignment. Can you do me a favor though?"

"Sure, what's up?" she responded, not sounding much like her normal self.

"Are you alright? You sound…"

"No, I'm okay," she said glancing back at the tub. "I just nearly drowned in the tub…"

"Really? Are you okay?" Trina reacted deeply concerned.

"Yeah, yeah, I'm fine? Let me guess the favor though. You need me to grab something to eat because it was your turn to cook tonight?"

"You got it," she laughed. "I left the money on the coffee table. You can't miss it."

"Anything in particular?"

"Nope, your call. Just hit me up when you get back home, so I know when to duck out of this unforgivably long near waste of time."

"Gotcha. Later." They ended the call, and Diana walked out of the bathroom and into the living room where she made herself a cool glass of water and flicked on the television set. The nightmare replayed itself in her head, but the more she became engulfed in the movie that was showing, the less she thought about it. It didn't take more than thirty minutes before she'd fallen back to sleep, only to awaken after three hours of napping before jumping up.

"Oh no," she yawned and stretched. "I have to go get dinner." She looked outside and it was already dark. "Dang." She grabbed her phone and texted Trina, letting her know that she was on her way to grab the food. "I hope she wants some fish because I sure do, so fish and veggies it is."

She dragged her feet back to her room to put on a sweat suit and sneakers, grabbed the car keys to her car that she called a used-mobile and headed out the door. She trekked down the staircase of the two story apartment building, noticing that the lights were out. "They know better than this. It's too dark. If I didn't know where I was stepping, I'd trip over myself," she complained. "One more thing to complain about in the morning to the staff. From snakes to their babies, I swear...we just need to move...and I have to walk blindly on this ground."

She tapped her right pocket for the mace she generally carried when she went anywhere, and then she tapped the left pocket for the stun gun. Then, she stopped in the middle of the sidewalk after noticing the night light at the bushes wasn't on either.

"You've got to be kidding me." She took her stun gun out of her left pocket and started walking past the huge bushes. She could see absolutely nothing, but it didn't matter to her at that point. If something jumped, she would stun it. It was just as simple as that. There was a golf course that left a large vast landscape of emptiness once clearing the bushes, and when Diana was in full view of it, she breathed a sigh of relief. Her car was only down the walkway a bit, so she continued to walk, not fast but cautiously. However, when she saw her car clearly, she picked up the pace, arriving to the car in full defense mode.

"Yes," she sighed, taking rapid, deep breaths as she tossed her stun gun onto the passenger's seat, hopped in the car, locked the doors and started it up. It was always a habit of Diana's to park facing out, so it took her no time to hit the gas and start the tires rolling. Her heart rate slowed and her paranoia left, causing her to smile again at the fact that she defeated her fears another day. Happily, she called her mom on speaker.

"Mom," she called as she heard her mom pick up on the other line.

"Hi, hon. Did you have a good day?"

"Sure did. On the way to get some food for tonight. Doing fish."

"Oh yeah? Is Trina with you?"

"No, she had to go to class for some project, but I texted her already so…" she continued, slamming on the brakes because she nearly ran a red light. The phone went flying onto the floor of the car. "Hold on, ma. Great, just great." She leaned over, attempting to find it by grazing her fingers over the car's floor fabric. Her mother called her name, but Diana yelled out louder. "Hold on, ma, I lost my phone." Frustrated, she looked up at the light, and it was still red. Therefore, she put the car in park and reached above her head to turn on the light. "Mi Dios!" she said in her native tongue as she leaned back over. Thankfully, she was able to pick it up just as the traffic light turned green. As she placed the cell phone into her lap and reached up to turn the car light off, she caught a glimpse of a body in the rear view mirror.

Diana instinctually reached for her stun gun, but there was no time as she screamed for her mom's help. She hit the emergency blinkers as she struggled to get loose from his strong grip while staring at his reflection in the mirror. He squeezed her throat until there was nothing left, and the name Dean was the last word that her mother heard her daughter say as Diana's head dropped onto the steering wheel, causing the horn to blare loudly into the phone.

Yet as Diana's car sat in the middle of the road at the traffic light, cars started to pile up behind her. Finally, people began to exit their cars, staring into the driver's seat, horrified by what they saw. Cell phones were in the air recording while some were dialing for help just as another car was coming from the opposite direction. The driver recognized the car and immediately pulled over on the side of the road. The passenger exited the vehicle and ran across the street, only to drop to her knees at what she saw. She cried viciously as she reached for the handle of the door, but when she couldn't get it open, she used the spare that was on her key ring. As she swung the door open, Diana dropped into Trina's arms.

Trina cradled Diana in her arms in the middle of the street, only listening to her mother cry on the other end of the phone. She knew that the man that only Diana could recognize had returned…and that he would go free. Dean was never found.

THE END

I Thought I Was Alone 3

"Hey, babe," she called taking a huge chunk from her apple as she sat at the small, glass kitchen table. "Did you see this?" she asked, spreading the paper out to get a clearer read.

"What about that paper? You know I don't read what's in the paper. If it's not on the internet or on the television news, then I guess I'm supposed to miss it," replied her husband as he fixed his neck tie at the stove where he was about to flip his grilled cheese sandwich.

"Tyrese, come here, no look," she called again, twisting her body to see him, but when he fell into her line of vision, she bolted from the table, dropping her apple on the floor. "Tyrese!"

"What?" he responded in shock by the sound of her call.

"Your tie!"

There was a glass of freshly squeezed lemonade filled with crushed ice, just like he liked it, sitting on the counter, and Charlotte wasted no time grabbing it and tossing over onto his shirt, soaking the flame that had already begun burning at the tie's tip.

"Your tie is on fire!" she screamed as she watched the lemonade and crushed ice soak into his dress shirt and slacks. "Was...it was on fire." She then scooted the empty glass back onto the counter.

"Dang! My suit!" he yelled, but glanced up at her gratefully at the same time.

"You're welcome," she stated.

"Yeah, thanks. Let me call them up really fast and tell them I'm gonna be running late," he stated, yanking his cell phone out of his pocket as he walked back to the bedroom, complaining under his breath. "I nearly burned myself up..."

"So much for the lemonade," she sighed as she walked over to the table leg to retrieve her fallen apple. There wasn't any visible dust on it, so she walked to the sink, rinsed it off and then took another bite. "God made dirt." She then quickly rushed back over to the newspaper where she'd become engulfed in a new story that had hit the front page.

She'd been on vacation for two whole weeks, and during that time, she pondered on how she would be able to establish herself more in the world of journalism. "This could be my ticket...this right here," she whispered to herself as she took another bite of the fruit, reading what she thought could possibly give her the story of a lifetime.

Pushing herself away from the table, she bit down into the apple in order to hold it inside of her mouth and walked back into the room with her husband, holding the paper open in both her hands. He'd already taken off his clothes by the time she reached their master bedroom and was rummaging through the closet to find another suit to wear while hanging up his cell phone. As soon as she saw his suit selection, she walked over, took it from his hands and began to touch it up with the iron.

"Sorry, Tyrese, baby, but you have to listen. Just sit there and read that story. It just happened yesterday, right outside the college campus. Sit! Read!"

"Charlotte, I'm late for work already."

"Just here," she stressed, waving her hand wildly toward the direction of the paper. "You already called them, and you're fine. That's my break out story," she continued, referring to the news article. "I'm going to make it my story. Watch. The headline…the headline!" she exclaimed as she began to remove the unwanted wrinkles from the top of his slacks and bottom of his shirt.

"Let me see what you're talking about," he sighed as he reclined his bare, dark-brown body on the bed to spread out the paper. "This is about that murder out there down the street from the campus, right outside of those apartments. Yeah, I read about this already on my cell. This was that breaking news. Why is this your ticket, as you call it, in journalism?"

"Do you really have to ask me that? You don't remember that name do you, of the girl they found at the scene, probably going freaking delirious? Her parents were filthy rich, and she was stalked when she was a teenager. It was a big deal, so big a deal that you have to remember. Everyone was talking about it."

He stared back at the paper, and then, she could tell by the way his eyes lit up that he knew exactly what she was talking about. "Oh, now I remember. That's the same girl, the exact same one that nearly got killed, right?" He located her name in the paper. "Trina. Trina Winslow, but it says Trina Winslow-Leets now. Yeah," he continued sitting up, even more interested in the story than previously. "My cousin knew her and her folks."

"Really? You never told me that?"

"Never knew it mattered. I don't know her, and honestly, I'm glad I don't. Seems like she attracts brutality." He tossed the paper over to the other side of the bed. "So how is something that's already reported going to end up being your discovery, my optimistic wife?"

"Well, I was thinking," she started, taking his slacks from the ironing board and tossing them over his way. He caught them and began to put them on as she continued, "I could locate her and get the full out scoop about her ordeal or, I should say, ordeals. At the same time though, I could even try and talk to that insane stalker, and maybe he'll lead me to where he got rid of her husband. The lunatic never said where or what he did with him. What do you think? No one has ever, and I mean ever, found his body. Plus, since the news is hot, this could easily make me front row for promotion!"

"Do what you have to do, baby, but I prefer you stay away from that quack job that left a slaughter at her house back in the day," he continued, zipping up his pants. "So, she found her friend dead right, like in the car?"

"Yes! Can you believe it? But get this," she continued, rushing over to her cell phone and typing in a search. "Not long before that, I think that she was also involved in another incident before she even got to this new campus. Basically, this girl is a trigger for bad luck when it comes to men...and friends. See, here it is right here." She fell atop the bed and tossed the phone right over into his lap. "She wasn't attending that school, but they mentioned her as the one attacked as she went to check on her cousin who ended up getting murdered in her own apartment. Isn't that weird? It's almost like death follows her or something."

"Unless she's the one planning it," he answered, taking in a deep breath of air as he put on his shirt and tie. "All of this stuff can't be coincidental, right? I mean, how many people nearly get butchered that many times in their lives. Sounds fishy to me. But look, I gotta go."

"Fishy? They investigated and all that. Don't you think they would have been able to pin something on her if she was involved?"

He shrugged his broad shoulders, and that was when she jumped right in front of him to kiss him good-bye. "Have a good day, and thanks for that other angle on this story. I didn't think about that, but I highly doubt she had anything to do with it."

"Never *not* doubt unusual stuff like that." He kissed her on the cheek, and she kissed him back on the lips. "I have to go, babe. I'm already late, and I make deadlines like I make love."

"How is that?"

"On point."

She kissed him once again, and as he turned to walk away, she pinched his butt. He laughed on the way down the hall. As soon as she heard the door slam, she immediately started to dial. She had to show up for work in one hour, however, she didn't want to waste time driving all the way there if she could get permission to start research on that new story right away. It would definitely make her boss proud while making herself more money.

"Hi, Mr. Matthews. This is Charlotte, and I'm sorry to bother…"

"Glad you called. I'm stuck in traffic, so I needed the conversation. Let me guess, you're stuck in traffic as well?"

"No sir… but I…"

"I hope not. Expecting you at work today because I have an event I want you to cover that's happening later on at three o'clock."

Charlotte rolled her eyes and dropped to the bed. She hated covering events. It was the worst thing possible for a journalist in her mind. She wanted to be the one to uncover what no man has ever done, and this was the case with Trina's story. For once, she wanted to be the one that broke the story, even if she had to play detective to do it.

"Well, I think I might have something far better than an event, Mr. Matthews," she continued, adding additional pep to her voice. "Do you recall that story that hit the headlines a year or so back maybe, about a stalker that broke out of the institution and ended up stalking a young lady by the name of Trina…uh," she stammered because the last name slipped her mind.

"Yes, I know exactly what you're talking about. She hit the news just twenty-four hours ago. A shame that girl. Can't seem to get it right. And this is your big story how? Do you know the killer to this recent tragedy because you know he's still out there? I mean, if you have information, you need to get to the office now so we can…"

"No, I don't. But I was thinking about going to interview her and the first killer from her teen years, just to see if I can break the case of where her deceased husband may lie. Plus, no one has done an exclusive with her since she's been an adult. It's like everyone has forgotten. This could be huge if I do it right, plus add fuel to finding this other murderer on the loose."

"It looks like you want to do something like a documentary, and then if possible, solve a case all on your own."

"Yes…yes. That's exactly right."

"Feel free. Just on your time. In the meantime, be at the event at three o'clock, understand? I expect you in the office as well. Oh and if you come up with some goods from your side job, and I mean real goods to be printed with your name in lights, well, let's just say, it will be good for not only you, but for all of us." After he spoke, there was nothing but the sound of horns blaring through the phone, until he started to talk again, causing Charlotte to hold her breath. "Now that I think about it, I'll give you an hour each day to research this project. We need something different." He hung up the phone.

"Hello? Hello? Mr. Matthews?" She pulled the phone from her ear, but when she saw that the call was over, she leaped atop the mattress and jumped all over the bed screaming. "I knew he would give it to me. I knew it!" Suddenly, she stopped jumping. "Crap! I have to get to work." In less than ten minutes, she was out the front door.

**

"This is boring as hell, Jazz," Charlotte complained as she sat in a seat as far to the back as she could get, holding her pen in one hand with her pad on her lap and tablet in the other hand while she spoke through her cell phone's ear piece.

"It could be worse. You could be working from home like me, hoping to get out and do something productive. Girl, I can barely move in here without taking some pain killers…and that only gives me relief for a couple hours until I have to pop another one. Gotta get this paperwork done and then run in to work for a sec."

"What are you working on?"

"Some of this and that. How about you? What's this event all about you're on?"

"It's this grand opening of the former governor's. You know, that big secret she'd proclaimed she would have in a couple years. Well, here it is…a restaurant. You'll read all about it with my name drowned out in the boredom of the whole article."

"Be quiet, Charlotte," Jazz giggled at her friend sounding so glum about her gig. "You are an excellent writer, and I'm sure you'll find something at the event to bring it to life. I'm willing to bet on it."

Charlotte sighed and said goodbye to her friend as she watched the former governor be chauffeured to the front of the restaurant. The chairs were in perfect assembly, and as the limo drove up, the crowd stood, forcing Charlotte up from her seat so that she could inspect everything from the governor's attire to the admiration of the onlookers who began clapping and whistling. Just then, a second car drove up and parked on the side of the new restaurant, and it caught most of Charlotte's attention because of the people who stepped out of the vehicle, one of which was her husband, Tyrese.

"Well, what do you know," she smiled as she whipped out her cell phone camera to begin taking photos of not only the governor and the restaurant, but also her dapper husband. "He is so damn confidential," she whispered as she continued to snap many photos of the event.

As she watched Tyrese walk to the front of the restaurant with the rest of the business men who apparently helped the former governor with this particular project, she lowered her camera as Tyrese began to scan the medium sized crowd that filled the parking area. It wasn't five seconds before he recognized his wife in the crowd, and Charlotte folded her arms, lifted her finger and shook it and her head with a huge grin on her face. Tyrese motioned an *I love you* back to her with his lips because he knew that she was going to jump on him about not telling her anything about the project before her boss did. Although she understood that he was sworn to confidentiality about clients no matter who they were, she also felt that he could have at least dropped the rules a little bit when it came to her. He never did, however.

Deciding to sit down and capture the event, she pulled out her notepad and began. She felt fortunate enough to get a jolt of excitement from Tyrese coming until it made her notes perkier and her overall mood about the event uplifted, however, every once in a while, her thoughts strayed to the Trina story and to another woman who seemed quite friendly at her husband's arm. Charlotte thought that she knew everyone who worked with Tyrese because she'd been to several luncheons and evening outings with him and his crew, however, this particular female had a very different demeanor than the others toward her husband.

Instead of getting too tangled up in what was going on publicly with Tyrese as he knew that she stood right there with the ability to cause a scene at a moment's notice, she shrugged off her paranoia and proceeded to take as many notes as possible so that her husband's secret project for the governor would get great coverage. There was only one other time that she'd coincidentally ended up on location with him, and she felt absolutely ecstatic about her current situation, altogether it making her job that much easier.

**

"So did you really have to do that, babe?"

"Do what?" he asked jokingly as she listened to him bite into what sounded like a juicy burger. Meat was

Tyrese's favorite food, so whenever he ate meat of any type, he would make sounds comparable to making sweet love.

"Not tell me anything about the secret project…like at all."

"No, no, no," he replied. "You can't hold anything to yourself. Next thing you know, the secret would have been out, and I would have been caught in the middle of it all being the project manager."

"Are you serious? You think I have mouth diarrhea?" she asked as she took a left onto the road that led to the psychiatric facility. She was on her way to see Stephen Evans, the man who escaped the facility a long while back and attacked the young lady who made the papers yet again that week, Trina. He'd been obsessed with her, according to reports and gossip, basically a stalking case, and it was in his path to her that many people were hurt, even killed.

"Do I? Baby, I love you and all. Never could replace you if I tried, but that mouth of yours. Don't make me choose between my career and you. I need money to pay these bills," he laughed.

"I know, baby, but that would have been a nice leak for me."

"That leak could have been traced back to me."

"You're right," she stated as she pulled onto the gated road surrounded by a plush lawn lined with red brick. "Well," she sighed, "I'm here."

"Where's that?"

"Oh, I didn't tell you, did I?"

"Tell me what?"

"I'm on my new job! Mine as in...my very own. I was able to pull many strings when I got back to the office, and I wound up setting up a meeting with Stephen Evans."

"Who is that?"

"The guy I was telling you about this morning."

"You weren't telling me about any guy this morning. You were telling me about Trina, that girl that found her dead roommate in the car on the road..."

"Yeah, well," she hesitated because she could hear the irritation in his voice about the whole meeting with Stephen Evans. She could tell that he'd already figured out what she was up to. "Stephen Evans is the man who is currently being rehabilitated after attacking Trina."

"If he's crazy, he's crazy, Charlotte. That dude could kill you and nothing be done about it as you sit right there with him talking."

"Tyrese," she tried to interject, but he stopped her with more arguing.

"You're taking this too far, Charlotte. Why can't you just interview the girl?"

"Because I already know her story, okay?" she shouted, feeling upset from his lack of support. "I just wrote a great article about the event that you kept secret from me, just to make you look absolutely great, and now I would appreciate the same support, Ty." She pulled up to the security guard who was sitting inside the booth, showed her credentials, and addressed him, "I have an appointment today with Dr. Cranizi, please. I'm from the paper."

"Are you really there?" Tyrese asked, shocked that she was serious about interviewing a psychopath.

"Yes, I am, Tyrese. You know what? Nevermind. I need a clear head while doing this, and right now, you're making it really freaking foggy. I love you and bye." Then she let out a huge scream in the car as the security guard looked on. She then glared back into his face after shoving her long blonde hair from her face. "It's fine. Man problems."

"You've come to the right place," responded the security guard with a smirk as he buzzed her inside. "Straight and follow the road to the right. Pull up to Building A. From there, follow what the board says on the right."

"Thanks," she sighed, feeling slightly embarrassed. As she pulled off, her face felt flushed, and when she looked into the rear view mirror, everything was verified. "Why can't he just support me this one time?" she complained. "Maybe I should just keep my projects to myself just like he does with his." Soon after she parked, her cell phone rang. It was Jazz calling her back about the new story she'd let her in on.

"Hey," Charlotte answered in a frustrated tone.

"Well, dog, Charlotte. Sound a bit more chipper being that you finally got a potential career breaking story on your hands."

"I am excited," she replied, putting the car in gear and grabbing her purse and notebook before exiting the car. "It's just that Tyrese thinks…"

"Oh, girl, stop. That's a man you got. He's supposed to protect you. Shoot, he isn't supposed to just be thrilled to know you're going to visit some psycho, now is he?"

"I guess not, huh?" She shut the door and gazed at the multitude of windows that lined the long narrow building.

"He's just so overprotective. I mean, this is my life, the career that I've always wanted. I don't want to just be a journalist. I want to be *the* journalist," she stressed.

"Well then go for what you know. If you get scared, keep me on the line," she joked. "Are you taking your headset?"

"Yep. I'm not that calm, cool and collected, Jazz, but I will definitely get through this." she laughed. "I have my recorder and everything. I want to break this story, so don't tell a soul."

"Girl, who am I gonna tell?"

"Thanks. You might be the only one to know anything else about this until it's over. I'm going mission nondisclosure with Tyrese from here on out."

"Do what you have to do. Get that story. He will feel good about it later."

"Bye." Charlotte turned off her ear piece and placed her cell phone on airplane mode so that it could be her second recorder just in case something happened to her primary one. Although her heart was thumping like a drummer on bass, she took in a relaxing breath and headed up the sidewalk toward Building A's entrance.

Just like the security guard explained to her at the gate, there was a bulletin that stated which direction she needed to turn in order to sign in. She followed the instructions until it led her to an enclosed central desk. There was no one else around besides the receptionist who was dressed completely in white from head to toe.

"May I help you?" she asked through the speaker.

Charlotte became startled at the security level of the place. She'd visited mental facilities before, but none that made visitors feel like an attack was imminent.

"Yes, I'm here to see Dr. Cranizi. I'm early...from the news..."

"I understand. Dr. Cranizi had me write you in. When I buzz, will you come through the door, please. Wait there, and I will open another door which is where I will meet you and take you to Dr. Cranizi's office."

Before Charlotte could say thank you, the receptionist was already gone. The next thing heard was the buzz, and Charlotte hopped toward the door, opened it and then ended up waiting for about ten more seconds before the next door was opened. As she stood there in solitude, she felt like she was being watched through the thick mirrors on both sides of her. Ten seconds felt like ten minutes as she forced herself to concentrate on the door in front of her. Closed spaces were never particularly friendly toward her ever since she was a child when her brother would lock her inside her closet as a prank. Finally, before the sweat started pouring down her forehead, the door opened, and she swiftly followed the nurse who appeared ready to mosey back to her front desk station. Before they even got to the end of the hallway, another health worker met them and led Charlotte further down the corridor until they reached the Dr. Cranizi's office.

"Thank you," Charlotte stated graciously to the male who escorted her to the proper office. The man nodded and carried on about his duties after knocking on Dr. Cranizi's office door, peeping inside and pushing the door open only slightly more.

It took no time for Dr. Cranizi to look Charlotte from her forehead to her feet as he remained seated at his desk.

His glasses were stylishly made for his face with an antireflective coating on the lenses so that one barely noticed the rimless mount of the frame. Although married, Charlotte nearly choked on her words at the sight of a handsome doctor that she assumed would be older and wiser in appearance. Instead, she got the opposite.

"Come in and sit please." He stood up as reached out to shake Charlotte's hand. "Mrs…"

"Middleton. Charlotte Middleton. I spoke with you earlier about Stephen Evans, your patient."

"I do remember, Mrs. Middleton. I do remember. Well," he sighed as he sat back down at the desk. "Evans, I think you should know before speaking with him, is a reader of the mind. Be careful what you say, how you say it, and make every attempt to move less than your normal movements."

"Excuse me?" Charlotte asked, not fully understanding what the doctor meant by her movements.

"You see, Evans has a high attraction, and once he finds something about you that he likes, it's hard to get him to detach. It's a good thing you aren't on television or I would have had to reject your request. However, being that you are more a writer in journalism, it should be much easier, that is if he engages with you, to disengage. Social media?"

Charlotte remained silent for a couple of seconds until she realized he was asking her about her social media status. "Oh…I'm sorry. Social media…just for work is all. No real pictures of me or anything, and if so, I can…"

"Delete them." He stared down at his work, but when he saw her not moving, he quickly looked back up. "Do you need to use my laptop?"

"Oh, now?" she asked, flushed with embarrassment while feeling like a small child in school on the very first day.

"Yes. Now...please. You see, Mr. Evans isn't as isolated as he was before, and we try to keep him away from habits to which he is accustomed to prior to his intervention. So far, he has been on the right track, but in one slip up, he will have gained access to every bit of your life, even from inside these walls. Our professionals at times aren't that professional all the time, especially when they want to keep silence and order, thus giving in to requests. Evans is charming but dangerous...as I'm sure you are aware."

Charlotte only stared at him. For such a handsome man, she couldn't fathom how he could be so stuffy. It almost made her giggle, but she held it in with a smile and a reach for her cell phone. "Let me double check my pics then...shant I?"

Dr. Cranizi ignored what he knew was a brief slight at him until Charlotte placed her phone back into her purse. It was in the very next second that Dr. Cranizi proceeded to move from his desk, and make his way to the door, stopping in front of Charlotte in order to be a gentleman. Charlotte removed herself from the chair quickly and prepared herself to meet the man responsible for several murders but getting punished for none. As she took a deep breath, Dr. Cranizi stepped in front of her before allowing her to exit. She stopped and stood there in front of him puzzled.

"I asked you to watch your movements, Mrs. Middleton. It is required."

"I didn't do anything, Dr. Cranizi."

"Practice your breathing. Stand here in front of me and just breathe. Get your rhythm and make it steady. You won't survive him if you can't survive me."

"Excuse me?" Charlotte asked feeling a bit offended.

"See what I mean."

Immediately, she realized how quickly she was thrown into a small fit of anger by the doctor and finally understood what she needed – a poker face but in more than just her face. She stared Dr. Cranizi in his eyes and began to breathe as he requested. He watched her deeply as she slowed her breathing down as far as she could. Then, he spoke to her, and when she returned words, he was pleased. She was finally relaxed. Dr. Cranizi glanced up at the clock that was on the wall.

"Good. Only ten minutes. And, Mrs. Middleton? I'm married as well. Not only that, but in love with her. I apologize if you took my stopping you at the door for flirtation. I'm only looking out for your best interests before we go any further. Like I said before, he is a charmer if he wants to be."

She nodded her head back at the handsome, six feet four inches tall, bald, brown-skinned and flawless psychiatrist and felt relieved. "Thank you...doctor. I apologize for my side comment back at the desk."

"It's quite alright. I never was one to care what anyone thought of me because I have always tended to think for them, if you understand what I mean. Follow me, and I will be right outside the door. Security will remain inside."

"Not. Not inside."

"Mrs. Middleton..."

"Please, I really don't want anything to leak. To be honest, I need a one on one...a true one on one. I'm not afraid."

"Security will be looking in through the window with his hand on the door. Remain seated. If the patient gets up, the interview is over. Fair enough?"

"Yes."

"I'm not here to protect you. I'm here to protect my patient, Mrs. Middleton. I'm protecting you in order to protect him. The danger you place yourself in is on you, not me."

"Understood," she fearlessly replied although it truly felt like a bowl of hot mush sat burning through her stomach lining. She thought about everything Dr. Cranizi stated about the man she was minutes from interviewing, and her blood pressure literally started to rise all over again. She felt a throb of anxiety all over herself, and when she reached the room where she would be left alone with the patient, her mind went blank as she stared into the empty space. "Where is he?"

"Please, have a seat. Familiarize yourself, and he will be coming in within two minutes. It's better you see him first versus him seeing you."

"You said he was getting better? Why all the formalities, besides the obvious reasons. I mean, is he going to attack me?"

"No. He won't...not today, and hopefully, no other day. Please, go in and sit."

Charlotte quickly grabbed her phone and turned on its recorder along with the hand held voice activated recorder that she placed on the table as soon as she sat in the chair which faced away from the freshly cut greens of the hospital yard. While in a fast attempt to regain her shaken focus, she saw him walking with a mental health specialist down the corridor. As he turned to walk inside the door, she began her breathing countdown. In less than three seconds, he was already positioned at his seat, sitting before her with an embracing smile on his face.

Charlotte decided to perform her movements, as if they were scripted. She thought before she acted each time, even when she reached out to shake his hand.

"Hello," she spoke to him as he simply stared at her hand in mid air.

"I'm being watched. I'm not allowed to touch you. Even animals are allowed to be pet, so I must be lower than an animal, don't you suspect?" he asked with what Dr. Cranizi would have labeled as a charming smile.

Charlotte suddenly understood exactly what Dr. Cranizi was talking about with Mr. Evans. He wanted to control the interview, but it was up to her to take the control back. "Mr. Evans, all living beings are precious. I'm glad that you agreed to this interview with me. My name is Mrs. Charlie Goodwin."

"Nice to meet you…Mrs. Goodwin. To what do I owe this pleasure. I don't have many beautiful blonds come my way often. They typically aren't my type, but I'm pleased to see you are very much atypical." His eyes didn't move from hers, and it was in that moment that she hesitated. Her breathing stopped only for a second but she was certain that he noticed. That didn't stop her.

"You're atypical as well. Tell me, Mr. Evans, about your infatuation with certain women, specifically Trina...Trina Winslow-Leets."

"Just Trina Winslow. Her husband is dead, or haven't you heard?"

"I have."

"Have you also heard that Trina belongs to me?"

"Does she? I haven't heard as of yet, but you just let me know, so I will make note of that."

"No need to make note of anything. You're recording it, so, stop with the pen...please. It shows your desire to be seen or known as the best to those who don't really understand that you already are...and slightly nervous. You haven't even written one word down yet."

"Okay, Mr. Evans. Tell me."

"Tell you what, Mrs. Goodwin? Is that your married name?"

"It is. Now tell me, Mr. Evans...your attraction."

"Trina was a nice girl. Rich but wanted to show how sweet she was underneath all that money. Most people with money are so...different. She was so revealing. She told me everything. We spoke regularly."

"Spoke?"

"Yes. Social media. She would post, and I could tell she wanted me to know where she was at all times. That night, I showed up to the party because her parents were going to be out of town. I knew she wanted me there."

"What about the night you showed up again, after she'd gotten married."

"Oh," he shivered but smiled. "That was the day she hurt me. She had another man taking care of our baby, so I had to take *our* baby. That man…"

"Creed."

There was a silence. It was the first time he looked away from her, and Charlotte pounced on the opportunity.

"You're looking at where you hid him, left him for dead?" she insinuated, believing that provocation would work best to get an answer from him, but before she could blink, his eyes shot back at her like he could leap across the table.

"What do you want?" he screamed as he beat his fists on the table.

"I want to know where you left Creed."

The guards immediately came through the door, and Mr. Evans began laughing hysterically, like his response and her question was all a joke. "Get off of me, please. I was teasing her," he said to the guards as he found Dr. Cranizi standing at the door. "Tell them. She's safe. I don't attack people I'm fond of," he continued, turning back to Charlotte.

The doctor nodded, and the guards let his arms loose. Dr. Cranizi was accustomed to his patient's mood swings and games. He did it to scare or annoy anyone who asked him something that he wasn't quite comfortable with in hopes that they would change the subject. Therefore, he wasn't prepared for what Charlotte said to him next as she sat there stone faced.

"Creed. Where is he?"

"Why would I tell you? Tell me this, did you happen to find out what happened to Trina lately? Is that what brought this whole interview about? She's locked up with me, isn't she? There's only one other place she could be."

"I'm not asking about her, Mr. Evans. I'm asking about Creed, her husband. He's been missing ever since he left home for work, and it was that day that you killed their baby and…" she continued as she watched his vein coil on the side of his temple. "Everyone just can't help but feel like you made him disappear. There's never been any proof, but everything points back to you, including, from what I read, your DNA in his car."

"Deoxyribonucleic acid. There was much on me that day, except for I don't know where Creed is. If I did, I wouldn't tell you…so that you can…"

"So that I can give the family some rest," Charlotte interjected. "It would give us all some rest, including Trina. She may even forgive you if you show some mercy, don't you think so?"

He quickly looked back at the doctor slightly amused, but then turned back to Charlotte with a stern and frustrated demeanor, like he was ready to pounce atop her and strangle the life from her lungs. Charlotte cringed just a little but stood her ground, leaning on the fact that if Mr. Evans did attack, she would more than likely survive with the strong arms of the guards backing her up along with her semi-mean left hook.

"Forgive me? Forgive me? I tell you what, *Mrs. Middleton*, since you want to play games," he snarled, causing Charlotte to cringe in her seat when he stated her real name. "Send a message to Trina for me, and I'll tell you what I know. Tell her I love her and if she wants to ever locate the man who she calls her husband, she'll have to talk to me herself. I'm done!" he yelled at the specialists to communicate that he was finished with the interview. "Be resourceful, *Mrs. Middleton*," he laughed, stressing her real last name again. "You were a liar coming in here, and I just made you an honest woman, didn't I, Mrs. Middleton? See you soon." he stressed with a smirk so harsh that it caused Charlotte to cave. She didn't know what to do as the doctor watched the mental health specialists whisk him away effortlessly.

Charlotte just sat there, shaking as if she wasn't looking into the eyes of another human being. The doctor noticed her shock and rushed in beyond the stalker who nodded to him and proceeded to his room. He went over and took a seat right up next to her, staring her in the face as she sat there, confused at what to say next, but knowing a choice had to be made – to take orders from Evans or leave her dream of potentially being an award winning journalist one day in the wind. One thing she had protecting her was the same thing the doctor had on his side – protecting her source. That she would do.

"What happened? You have to tell me because…" he asked

"Nothing. Nothing happened. I'm upset though because he refused to tell me anything. He told me that he would meet with me again." She looked into Dr. Cranizi's eyes. "He chose to meet with me again and that will be when he'll continue the interview. It was his choice, so I accepted. I was annoyed," she continued pushing back her chair, "But I accepted. I figure I can get a fairly good story out of him if he trusts me enough to talk."

"Mrs. Middleton," he called as she walked away from him, purposely refusing to face him.

"Yes?" she responded, turning to look into her purse instead of at him.

"Don't give him leverage. He will take it." He paused to await a response from her, but when he got none, he escorted her out, beyond his office and to the security doors. The whole way back, Charlotte couldn't believe what she was about to do, but it was exactly what Evans wanted, to talk to Trina.

**

"That was great, wasn't it?"

Caught off guard, Tyrese spun around to come face to face with his new co-worker as he walked toward the building where he made his career for seven years.

"Oh yeah, it was great. Patrice, right?"

"Got it on the first try. You remembered."

"It's a gift of mine."

"How so?"

"Well, you think of something that helps you remember a person's name as soon as you meet them, associate the person with something you like, dislike, or doing something as simple as repeating the name continuously in your head while the person is standing before you," he stated as she joined him walking toward the entrance from the parking garage.

"Which one was it?"

"Pardon me?"

"How you remembered my name?"

"Uh…" he grinned, feeling the hint of flirtation going on from the young lady's end. "Let's say I just remembered your name. Ladies first." He held the door open for her, and she walked in slowly. To Tyrese, her slow gait felt like forever because he couldn't take his eyes off of her. She was a highly attractive female, and as he followed behind her, he knew she was the temptation that would eventually lead him away from his wife once again.

"Thanks, Tyrese. So, how long did it take to get that project completed?"

"It's been months now actually. The governor changed her mind on a couple of things throughout the process, but in the end, we drew up the plans and got things going for her nicely, trying to integrate her style with the viewpoints of the public to make a nice flowing atmosphere for everyone to enjoy. Did you like the final product?"

"Sure did like it. You did a great job."

Tyrese looked away and smirked, becoming grossly involved with the conversation. He'd already cheated on Charlotte a multitude of times before, most of them of which she wasn't aware. Although he was going to try not to do it again, he knew it was highly likely that he would lose the battle.

"Listen up, though. I have a date…with my wife…so I have to take the stairs because I'm already late," he lied. "Take it easy, Patrice."

She smiled back as she pushed the elevator button. "Yeah, you take care."

"No problem doing that, Patrice. No problem," he responded, shaking his head in the process as he walked through the door that led to the staircase and ran up.

Climbing stairs quickly was like a warm up exercise. He was very built, working out about four days a week in one of their bedrooms which they converted into an indoor gym. When he reached the entrance to the fifth floor, he took a deep breath, shook off the flirtation only for a moment, and walked confidently to his office. He knew he was a fool for even entertaining the thought of trading the woman who was there for him through thick and thin in exchange for the woman he knew no longer than the new watch on his wrist. Even that would stop ticking and let him down before Charlotte would, and he truly believed that, however, he doubted those facts would stop him from doing something he'd become so accustomed to doing – being with other women, if only for one night.

Upon walking into his office, there was something on his desk that he hadn't left there before leaving - a pink greeting card. Figuring that it was from the woman he needed to hear from the most after his encounter, he smiled and waltzed over to it while sitting at his desk. As he opened the envelope and pulled out the card, his cell phone rang.

"Hello?" His eyes glanced over the card, and immediately stopped at what was taped to the inside. "Hey, baby, uhhh… what's this about?"

"What are you talking about?" Charlotte asked curiously.

"What am I talking about? Oh, oh…no, no. I was talking to a co-worker. Let me call you right back, baby. As a matter of fact, I'm leaving now." Before Charlotte even said good-bye, he ended the call, dropped the card and pushed himself away from the desk with a huge grin on his face. The key was to a hotel room and the time read nine o'clock at night along with the aroma of a sexy perfume. The only thing wrong with the invitation was that it wasn't from his wife. The invitation spelled that out with three words – *not your wife*.

He felt trapped in temptation as he turned toward the huge window that allowed him to see the freedom of the outside world. "Who the hell is this?" he questioned himself quietly as his thoughts went to the new co-worker named Patrice who he just attempted to brush off in the parking garage although he had no real proof of where the anonymous gifts and invitations were coming from. That card on the desk wasn't the first time he'd received something from someone unidentified. It had already happened several times before. Some he followed up on while some he didn't.

After pondering over the offer, he turned back around at his desk, picked up the card, ripped it to shreds, and tossed it in the trashcan along with the key. As he picked up his cell phone to call Charlotte back, he thought about it once again, then retrieved the very thing he just tore up. He searched through the torn pieces of paper until he saw the room number and hotel. Then, he memorized them while stuffing the key in his pocket. Afterwards, he leaned back in his chair, inhaled and returned the phone call to Charlotte, his mind racing about what he'd planned on doing until his thoughts were interrupted my her voice.

"I see you beat me here."

He hung the phone up just as Charlotte's cell phone rang. It was Patrice.

"Didn't know it was a race. May I help you with something?" he asked, but knew exactly what she wanted. It was evident from the first time they spoke, and it was very obvious that she didn't mind he was married.

There she stood at his office door wearing a red dress with cleavage obviously readjusted for his eyes and her hand on her hip to accentuate her curves. Tyrese was impressed that she'd gone through all the trouble to readjust what was already good enough for him to admire. He could tell she wasn't an amateur at what she was doing because the word wife didn't scare her away at all. She'd been down that road before and knew the unspoken rules.

"Before you leave to meet *her*, will you approve something for me?"

He grabbed his keys and walked toward the door, but Patrice stood her position, smelling like a batch of fresh flowers. "I need to close my door…and lock it," he stated firmly as she stood there dissecting his hormones the best that she could.

"Alright," she sighed, looking down disappointed but then snapped out of her saddened gaze to look back into his eyes with a bright smile. "See you later then?"

"I got your key," he responded, relieved it was her.

"Good."

Tyrese watched her walk away from the door and down the hall, and there was no doubt she was doing her best to keep his attention. Finally, he turned around, and walked toward the exit. It was then that he turned back to look once again. She was there, looking back at him, so their eyes met. Instead of waiting another second, he pushed the door and walked down the staircase. Not soon after, he pulled the hotel key from his pants pocket and rubbed it in between his fingers. Then, he proceeded to move towards his car, got in, and drove.

**

Charlotte sat on the toilet, placing her head into her hands. "What have I done?" she moaned. Ever since she left the mental health facility, she was shaken by the fact that Stephen Evans knew who she really was. He had her made at the first hello. "Jesus," she panted. "I feel like throwing up." She quickly fell to her knees and turned around to face the toilet just in time. Vomit filled the bowl, and when she finished regurgitating her nerves, she weakly reached over her head and flushed.

Falling backwards onto the tiled floor, she realized she really needed to talk to someone, but when she called Tyrese, he rushed her off of the phone. When she called Jazz, she didn't pick up the phone at all.

"It wasn't supposed to happen like this. I was supposed to use a fake name, a freaking fake name, and now…" She didn't even complete her sentence before she knew that eventually that would have been impossible, but at least he would have found out her real name after the publication, not before. It left her terrified that a real killer knew things about her that she had no idea he knew. As she sat there on the cold bathroom floor, fully dressed and nearly in tears although she'd already decided to push through the chaos, she heard the sound of keys at the front door.

Quickly, she jumped up from the floor, took a deep breath and gargled with some mouthwash after running the toothbrush across her teeth. Then, she tossed some water onto her face to make an excuse for her flushed appearance, and as she heard her husband walk inside and shut the door, she swallowed her fear. She decided to keep the worst parts of the interview with Evans a secret.

"Hey, baby? Are you home?" he asked being that he came in through the front door and didn't check the garage.

At first, Charlotte didn't answer him because even though she had a mental plan, the rest of her body didn't want to follow. Because of that, she reached over and locked the bathroom door before shouting, "I'm in the bathroom!" From there, she turned on the shower and undressed. "I'll be out in a minute." As she stepped inside the tub, she heard him shake the bathroom door handle.

"Babe, what's wrong with you? Why did you lock the door?"

"Nothing's wrong. I just locked the door is all. Interviewing a psycho makes you kind of nervous, you know, so locking the door was the perfect way to keep safe from my imagination, right?" she replied, grateful that she was able to think fast. He was right. She never locked doors inside the house.

"I told you not to do that interview. What did I say?" he boasted, continuing to walk down the hallway as he realized he left the hotel key in his pocket. Before he heard Charlotte respond, he jogged back outside, careful not to slam the front door, and slid the hotel key inside his glove compartment. Then, he slipped back inside the house and eased by the bathroom door to get into his workout clothes before heading to the workout room.

His mind was all a whirl, but he maintained his composure as he heard Charlotte exit the shower. With his headset on, he turned the volume up in order to drown out her voice as he considered doing something that he'd convinced himself on the way home would be the very last time. Charlotte, on the other hand, was making every effort to drown out her fears and walk through the fire she'd made for herself to come out unsinged.

As she exited the bathroom, she was shocked to not find Tyrese in the bedroom. She slid on a change of clothes and pulled her hair into a high bun that sat directly on the center of her head. She stared at herself in the mirror, and then spotted her purse sitting there on the corner of the dresser. She reached in and put a new lock on her cell phone while taking the tape recorder out as well to hide it not only inside her sock drawer, but inside a pair of socks. The last thing she wanted was for Tyrese to listen to it and find out that things were too close for comfort than what he wanted.

As she examined herself in the mirror, she practiced smiling as naturally as she could until she was satisfied. The tears of doubt and the unknown wanted to fall, but she had to dismiss her fear and move toward her goal. The odds of anything happening to her was low, but just the thought made her cringe. Just knowing a maniac knew information about her, and possibly even her spouse, crept her out just enough to consider dropping the ball on everything, but Evans promised. Therefore, she would hold him to it and pray everything worked out just fine.

Exiting the bedroom, she put a pep in her step, attempting to transform into her usual upbeat self when she entered the makeshift gym to give her husband a pleasant hug and kiss on the cheek as he lifted his weights.

"Finally, I get to see you, and you're all sweaty and ready, just like I like you," she smiled through her anxiety, relieved that he didn't immediately notice anything unusual. "So what was that all about?"

"What was what all about?" he asked back, already having planned to divert the conversation if she asked about why he'd gotten off of the phone earlier. "And watch out now, I don't want to hit you with these on accident. I told you about walking up on me with these bells in my hand. It's dangerous."

"You wouldn't hit me on purpose, so that's good enough for me."

"Not for me though." He placed the weights down and turned to take her in his arms and give her a warm, gentle kiss. As he did, images of Patrice formed inside his head, and he pulled back, pretending that he had a sore neck. "Man, I must have strained myself back here," he continued rubbing his neck and shoulders. "Do we have any of that uh…"

"Ointment?"

"Yeah, that stuff. It works wonders. I thought we had some, but…"

"No, that's all out. I can run and get you some if you…"

"No, as a matter of fact, I'll run out and get some later. How about that interview though?" he asked, grabbing a towel and wiping his face down and around his neck.

"Well, it went well…actually," she stammered. "I didn't get what I was looking for, but I got enough for a second interview. I'm setting up an interview with Trina if I can, too."

"So soon after the attack?"

"Yeah, I want it while it's fresh. I realize if she is admitted, they may not allow it, but hopefully, Trina will accept. She's an adult now versus when she was a kid, so…no need for parents at all. They're a journalist's worst nightmare sometimes. On top of that, I think she may just be admitted for follow up counseling versus the whole shebang of going back into a severe depression. At least that's what people are saying."

Right after her words, instead of more prompting from Tyrese, there was a deafening silence, like an overwhelming tension that she'd discerned a few other times before. She believed it was Tyrese wanting her to divulge information, but that particular time, her discernment of him was quite wrong. His mind had wandered once again to Patrice, and just like the other times, he had a hard time shutting his sexual addiction down, an addiction that Charlotte knew nothing about. Only a couple of hours after that conversation, Tyrese was gone and Charlotte was believing the fabrication that he had to numb his pain with an over-the-counter ointment.

** **

Dialing Jazz's phone number, she looked at the clock. It was eight-thirty on the dot. The evening came in quietly, and as it continued, Charlotte became calmer about her situation. All she had to do was figure out a way to get to Trina soon so that she could be the journalist responsible for breaking a murder mystery.

"Come on, Jazz, pick up. I have got to tell you…"

"Hello?"

"Jazz, I'm so glad you answered. Listen up. You know I went on that interview today right, and…"

"Hold up a second, Charlotte." There was the sound of ruffling that sounded off into the phone, and mixed with it was the sound of distant voices. "Yeah, I'm back."

"Where are you? You sound like you're out and about."

"Girl, I am…but Charlotte, I gotta go. I'll call you later. Bye," she stated, rushing off of the phone while leaving Charlotte in a funk.

"So much for that conversation," she thought to herself as she scrolled through her telephone to check social media while she hopped atop her bed, kicking her legs up in the air in search of Trina's social media account. "I know she has one. She must. I just have to find it. Hospital or not, this generation lives to talk on the web, stalker or no stalker." Her scroll and search was interrupted, however, with a call from Tyrese.

"Did you make it to the store yet?" she asked without having to wait on him to say hello.

"Yeah, I'm getting ready to walk inside now. My boss called me though, baby. I'm gonna have to stop by the office for some emergency planning with him. I don't know how long it's gonna take either, but if you need me for something, just text or call. If I can't pick up, I'll call you right back."

"Again? Can't it just wait until tomorrow?"

"Apparently not, Charlotte, if he called me in with a couple other people tonight. Let me go make this money without you feeling like you're missing out on me. Got me feeling guilty," he joked. "Hey, baby?" he stopped her before she ended the call. "I love you. See you tonight." Once he heard the phone call end, he proceeded down the road in his Lexus. "Now, let's see where I can park at this hotel," he sighed as he glanced around the parking garage area making certain that there was no one around that could identify him. He'd never been to that particular hotel before, but going on a liaison in a strange place never bothered him. He just knew to keep his head down and take the stairs to whatever room he was going toward. Simple solution to not being detected in the vast lobbies.

Pulling into the parking spot, he decided to back in so that no one would see his license plate. Then, he checked the glove compartment for the key, and sure enough, it was exactly where he'd left it. "Room 459. Time to go meet you, Ms. Patrice," he said looking at his cell for the time.

He opened his door and stood up, allowing himself time to scope the place out. When he didn't see anyone in front of him, he turned to close and lock his car door and that was when he saw the image of a female standing almost directly behind him in the reflection of the tinted window. Not startled much by the presence of a female, he turned around to speak with his flashy smile, but there was no one there.

"The hell?" He turned to look back at the reflections of his window, but there was still no one there. "Must be seeing things," he laughed. "Paranoid as hell tonight. Feel like people watching me," he joked, finally turning toward the hotel's side entrance. Once more, he searched the area around him and even inside nearby cars, but didn't see any woman there. Everything was quiet, so he turned his cell phone on silent and continued toward his abominable destination. While the cell phone was in his hand, he set an alarm on his phone to remind him to stop at the store and get the ointment that he lied about needing.

As he walked, he also thought up an arrangement of lies that made sense so that Charlotte would never second guess it. She was good at what they both called *sensing sin*, and she'd had much practice being with him despite her never figuring out even half of the dirt he'd done behind her back. He wasn't proud of it, but he just couldn't help himself, something he jovially considered a lack of boyish discipline in the grown man world he'd built around himself to cover it up.

Before he walked inside, there was another odd noise behind him, causing him to stall and look. Once again, he saw no one, but began to grow increasingly paranoid as he used the key entry to open the side door and enter the long corridor. From there, he located the staircase which he used to take him to the fourth floor.

The time on his cell phone read five minutes after nine o'clock, and when he walked to the room, he placed his ear up against the door. There was total silence. He looked back and forth down the hallway as he slid the key into the rectangular slit and pulled down on the handle. Then, he stepped inside, allowing the heavy door to close behind him.

It was obvious that his night was going to be good. He may not have seen the woman, but he saw her preparation. The sheets were already pulled back with her red lingerie on the bed, but as he turned toward the small closet, expecting to see her, there was no one there. Finally, he sat on the bed where he zoomed in on a bottle of champagne with a note that stated *I'll never leave you lonely, Tyrese.*

"It looks like you're leaving me lonely right now, though," he smiled, feeling good about the night as he waited on Patrice to walk into the room, figuring that he was in for more of a treat than what he thought. "This is different." He stood back up, walked over to the mirror that was attached to the bathroom door and looked himself over. "You in here, Patrice?" he asked, as he knocked once and then one more time as he listened for a reply. Finally, he decided to go inside slowly. "I'm comin' in. No need to put on those clothes because I'm sure you look good without them," he complimented her as he walked inside.

The bathroom was warm and humid, leaving a heavy mist over the mirrors. Immediately, he removed his shirt and pants as he heard the sound of water dripping inside the tub, ricocheting off of a tub full of water. He knew she was inside awaiting him. "Your sexy ass," he continued to speak as he wiped his face one time from his forehead to his chin, and as he pulled back the heavy shower curtain and stepped inside, he fell backwards against the wall, hitting it excruciatingly hard as his eyes fell upon the bloodiest sight he'd ever seen. "Shit! Oh, shit!" His hand slipped, and he fell against the toilet, sending him slamming his naked body to the floor, the bloody water splashing everywhere as Patrice's sliced body continued to gush blood from her stomach and face. Her face was mangled, and her body was torn open while up above her was a note attached to the tile that read *Not so beautiful anymore, now is she?*

Tyrese plastered his hand against his body to try and forcefully wipe blood off himself as he turned to face the bathroom door, afraid that he would be caught off guard by the killer and sliced up just like the woman he barely knew. "Fuck!" he panicked as he pulled the white towel from the hanger and wiped his legs and body as hard as he could. Blood continued to find its way onto his body, so he stood up from the floor and moved toward the sink. About to wipe the mirror, he suddenly stopped, his heart pounding as he shot a glance back at the deceased who floated there in the tub with her mouth and eyes wide open. Then, he placed his hands in front of his face and nearly vomited in the toilet. Fortunate for him, he was able to hold it down as he dropped the towel to the floor and shoved the towel across the floor vigorously with his foot to erase any trace of his fingerprints. He then put on his clothes as he ripped another towel from the holder and wiped everywhere he thought he'd touched.

Tyrese could barely breathe, so with the towel, he opened the door once again and let the cooler air inside before he exited. Three seconds hadn't gone by before his eyes darted over to the champagne bottle. Believing he would faint at any moment or even worse, lose control of his bowels, he ran toward the bottle of champagne and ripped the note from the string. "Damn!" he shouted as he removed his hand from the bottle. His fingerprints were all over it, so he took the bottle with him as he bolted from the door.

"Hell with this. Jesus, if you get me out of this, I promise I'll live right. I won't cheat again, and I will live right," he said choking back his tears and fears as he raced down the hallway with his head completely down as not to get captured by any cameras. As soon as he hit the parking garage, he lifted his eyes only slightly as to locate his car and notice any patrons. There were none, so instead of keeping a heavy walking speed, he began to run because his freedom depended on it. As he turned toward his car, he paused, and just like someone had a pistol to his head, dropped to his knees. He wanted to shout out loud, but he covered his mouth and groaned ferociously as he placed his head down to the ground in order to fight back his fear and anger at the same time. His front tire was flattened with a bloody knife jammed directly inside it.

The deeply masculine voiced Tyrese sounded more like a weeping bird as he sounded off, "I can't...I didn't do it. I didn't..." Through all his groveling however, he didn't give up. He crawled to the knife that jutted out from the tire and pulled it out, but he knew he couldn't put it on the ground anywhere because of his fingerprints. He had nowhere to wipe it down either besides his shirt, and he needed the shirt to not look suspicious to Charlotte when he returned home.

"Damn!" He finally shouted as oncoming car lights began to shine in his direction from a car that was entering the garage. Quickly, he opened his car door and sat in the driver's seat, hidden by the heavily tinted windows as the car headed toward him before it turned right to head in another direction. Holding the knife in the palm of his right hand, he searched his car for anything to lay it down on, but as usual, his car was spotless with nothing useless laying around. Therefore, he switched it over to his left hand, started the car and put it in gear to drive. With his foot nervously on the brake, he listened for any sirens, and when he didn't hear any, he pulled off, his car leaning to the side and wobbling toward the street. As he exited, another car pulled in. Both drivers locked eyes, but the cars continued to roll toward their destinations.

As Tyrese rolled slowly down the street, he turned his rear view mirror toward the parking garage so that he could determine whether or not the car that pulled in didn't turn back around to trail him. When it didn't, he stepped on the gas to find the nearest twenty-four hour drug store because he knew his car wouldn't make it back home, much less too much further down the road. The last thing he needed was for a police officer to stop him. Soon enough, he saw a drug store and pulled into the parking lot.

"That's what I'm gonna do. Just go to the drug store like I said. Yeah…" he panted, almost wheezing, as he convinced himself that everything was going to be fine. As he pulled up, he stopped just short of the building's video camera and parked. The knife that he held onto the whole time he drove his three wheeled car down the road, remained in his hand as he opened the door. Then, he placed it adjacent to his leg.

Where he'd parked, no one was on the driver's side of his car. Instead, there was a small tree that was erected in the center of the bushy greenery. It became the perfect cover for him as he rushed toward the trashcan before any patrons came near him or his car. The trashcan was where he dumped the bloody knife in hopes that it would be taken to the back dumpster at closing time without anyone getting injured, thus discovering it. That would be a link back to him through fingerprints that he just didn't want to imagine.

From there, he took a deep breath as he walked down the sidewalk. Someone exited the drug store and was coming straight towards him. This made his heart go into what felt like convulsions, and he suddenly felt faint, so faint that he leaned against the brick wall. All he could see was Patrice's dead body lying in a literal pool of blood. It was that alone that was about to make him spiral out of control.

"Sir, sir, are you alright? Can you stand up?" asked a concerned older woman with her cell phone in her hand about to dial 911. "I can call…"

Tyrese rushed to stop her, quickly regaining his composure. "No, no ma'am. I just saw a doctor at the emergency room. I'm picking up my meds now. Should feel better really soon. Just a case of pneumonia got me weak in the knees tonight."

"Well, get in there and sit down. I'll wait on you to get in good. Go on."

Tyrese didn't respond in words, but he only nodded and continued walking, trembling in his gut. Shoving his hands into his pockets as the sliding door opened, he didn't think twice about looking back to see if the woman was still watching. He just walked inside and headed straight for the bathroom.

"Oh God," he vomited through a string of prayers for the Lord to help him. The toilet felt like it was floating instead of water floating in it. Soon, Tyrese was on the floor, sprawled out in a daze until there was a knock on the bathroom door.

"Anyone in here?" asked a commanding voice.

Tyrese jumped from the floor and quickly answered, "Yeah, I agree. I mean, I'm coming out...right now." He then flushed the toilet and exited the bathroom to find that the man who spoke to him was already walking away. From there, Tyrese hustled to the shelf and grabbed the ointment. "Shit!" There was a streak of blood on his hand originating from the knife, and it wasn't his blood, but Patrice's. It looked even redder when it smeared across the white box of ointment.

His heart sunk, and it felt like a huge bowel movement was churning in his stomach. His strong chest shrunk as he debated on leaving the ointment in the store and grabbing another, however, it was too risky. He felt like all eyes were on him, and if a camera was on him, they could easily match him to the blood stained ointment tube on the shelf. Fear entered into his mind even more, but he finally reached the counter after wiping the blood stained ointment box clean on his pants.

"Ten dollars and fourteen cents, please."

"Aren't you gonna scan it?"

"You're bleeding, sir, so no," the attendant stated clearly frustrated as she leaned down to bust open a fresh pack of gloves. "Please say debit."

"No, it's cash." She rolled her eyes as he scooted the money on the counter.

"Sorry."

As he walked out the door, he overheard the cashier shouting, "Will somebody come put this money in the bag for me? I'm not touching it at all so..."

Her voice faded as he approached his vehicle, and then he looked at the time. Planning everything out in his head, he opted to call Charlotte and tell her that he wasn't going to make the fake meeting at his job because someone sliced his car tire open at the drug store.

"Yeah, yeah," he answered the thoughts in his head as he sat inside his car. "No, no!" he continued, slamming his hand against the steering wheel. "My rims are messed up. Shit. My rims are all jacked up." He knew there was no way Charlotte would believe the story of the car tire getting slashed at the drug store just because the rims were obviously destroyed from having been driven on. "I got it. I got it." He began to dial.

Each number on the cell phone felt like needles stabbing his fingertips, and when his wife answered, his tongue froze as he sat there needing help but not knowing what to say without being caught in the act, no matter what he said.

"Hello? Tyrese?" Charlotte called into the phone.

"Yeah, baby, I'm here. I'm here."

She heard the uneasiness in his tone, causing her to become extremely pointed with the next words to flow from her mouth. "What's wrong? I can already tell, Tyrese. You don't sound right at all."

"Uh, I'm about to call a tow because I don't know…I don't know what happened…I uh…"

"Tyrese, what?" she yelled out of concern. "Stop playin', and just say it. Are you okay?"

"I'm okay, but I'm trying to figure out what I hit."

"Hit? Oh my goodness."

"Yeah, I was just driving, just down the street from the drugstore when something slashed my tire. My rim and all is torn up."

"Nobody got hurt, right, Tyrese? Please tell me no one got hurt," she started to panic.

Someone was hurt, and that someone was Patrice in the bathtub. Tyrese's mind spun around and around as he continued to stare at the blood he wiped on his pants.

"Tyrese?"

"Oh yeah, baby, I was just looking at something. My tire is ripped apart, and I'm gonna wait here for help."

"What drugstore are you at so I can come get you?"

"Baby, you don't need to come out here."

"Tyrese?" she asked confused, assuming there was something else going on. "I'm coming to get you," she said firmly. "Where?"

"That twenty-four hour drugstore," he sighed, "The one on Manillo Avenue, across from the park – Youth Park."

"Youth Park isn't anywhere near your job, Tyrese? Why did you go in that direction when there are plenty drugstores…"

"Just that's where I am, Charlotte," he snapped, shutting down Charlotte's line of questioning, but as soon as he did it, he realized what he'd done and apologized. "I'm sorry, baby. I'm just stressed out is all. First, I miss my meeting and now this."

Charlotte accepted his apology with reservations. "Love you. Be there as soon as I can." She didn't believe him. She'd been in the situation before, where she would get hit with harsh words for doing absolutely nothing. It was the sign of another woman, and even though she tried to get it out of her system, the thought remained lodged there in her head as she made her way to where he was stranded.

Time drifted nowhere as Tyrese sat inside his car watching cars drive by in his rear view mirror. The street wasn't too busy, but paranoia engulfed him because the uneasiness of someone watching him never went away. The fact was that someone was watching him, and whenever the cars stopped at the traffic light, his heart raced. Was he the next to die? He began to dial, the phone started to ring and after the first ring, someone picked up.

"Yo!" a jovial guy hollered into the phone. "Tyrese!"

"Hey, man, listen. You busy?"

"Yeah, why? You not watchin' the game?"

"No, I'm stuck. My tire got slashed man."

"I knew that shit was gonna catch up to you, man," he responded, referring to his friend's affairs.

"No, no, nothing like that. I mean, something in the road slashed that thing up on the way to the drugstore. Man, I even got cut trying to inspect it, blood all on my hand and everything. Can you do me a solid?"

"After the game. I already know what you want me to do. I'll get it tonight after the game. Text me…"

"No, get a pen and write it down."

"What?" his friend replied a bit annoyed. "I just told you I'm watching the game. Text me where it is, and I'll haul it in tonight or first thing in the morning. You alright, man?"

"Yeah, my bad. Thanks, man. I'll tip you nicely."

"Alright, bro."

The call ended, and just like that, he saw a car move past the rear of his car slowly. Quickly, he turned around in his seat to see who it was staring directly at him, but he couldn't see anything more than an outline. Instead of just sitting in the car, he felt the need to defend himself from the unknown, so he shoved his car door open and charged the person inside the car like a madman. Before he reached the trunk of the car, the driver pressed firmly down on the gas and the car sped off, darting back into the traffic as if the only person on the road.

Tyrese chased the car until he could chase it no more and finally stopped to catch his breath, pondering what his next move was. As scenarios rushed through his head, he reached his car to only see Charlotte pull up in the next five minutes.

On the way back home, they barely spoke, and the next couple of days that passed were spent in silence. Charlotte could barely look at Tyrese nor sleep underneath his warm body as she was accustomed to doing because of the adulterous thoughts that bombarded her. As soon as she got him home that night, he constantly checked his cell phone. Even when they were lying down in the middle of the night, she would see the light come on underneath the covers, and she fumed. Still, she decided to ignore him and focus on the job she decided to place above him and his flat tire.

Divorce continued to play out in her head because cheating was something she could no longer stomach, but before she could do that in the way she wanted to do it, she needed to go full force with the one thing that could push her salary to the highest it had ever been. Doing that would mean following through on the interview that she made while Tyrese became too preoccupied to care – her interview with Trina. It was in a couple hours.

Instead of eating in the kitchen with Tyrese who attempted the smallest amount of chatter he possibly could with her, she sat in the living room and turned on the television. Being a journalist, she already knew what was going on for the most part and what was also getting ready to happen, but when she flicked on the news, there was something brand new and tragic to hit the screen.

"A bloodbath, literally, was found at the Keystone Hotel when a woman was discovered in the bathroom of her hotel room with multiple stab wounds and her body mutilated. Police stated that the body had been there for at least two days, and while the police are still investigating, they say that they have yet to find any leads to what they describe as a gruesome homicide. More on this story at six. In other news..."

Right after the news hit Charlotte's eyes and ears, she picked up her cell phone to dial in to work to find out who was on it. That was when she caught a glimpse of Tyrese behind her staring at the television as if he'd seen a ghost. For two days he hadn't shaved as well as he normally did, leaving small patches of roughness on his face, as if he didn't even see them there. As Charlotte stared into Tyrese's eyes and then back at the television, Tyrese didn't flinch. It was as if he was still watching them talk about the woman who was murdered despite the fact that another, far less captivating story was being reported.

"Tyrese," she finally shouted purposely, causing him to nearly jump from his skin. He stared back at her, his mouth gaped open like he had something to say, but instead of saying it, he kept quiet, shutting his mouth, taking a deep breath, and answering.

"Yeah, yeah…baby listen. I'm not going in to work today. Not feeling too good at all. Gonna check on my car. It should be fixed."

"What the hell is wrong with you? You act like I don't know? And then you walk around here quiet as hell, checking your damn phone in the middle of the night," she yelled as she reached over and punched the phone from his hand. It hit the floor and slid towards the kitchen. "How dare you? And where's that ointment? Did you get it before or after you slept with her?"

His eyes shifted like a lost man's or like a man who was being followed. Tyrese appeared not only fearful but insecure as Charlotte continued talking, darting the worst questions at him and answering them as if he couldn't answer them himself. His mind began to spin until he shouted.

"I didn't sleep with anyone! I didn't fuckin' sleep with anybody. I went to the damn drugstore, Charlotte, alright? The fuckin' drugstore, dammit!" He turned and swung his fist so hard that he punched a hole into the freshly painted wall, causing a big chunk to fall onto the floor. Then he stormed to the back room and shut the door, leaving Charlotte alone to fume, yearning for a way to prove his infidelity because she couldn't take his lies anymore. As she sat in solitude, her phone rang. She allowed it to ring three times before answering. It was Jazz.

"Yeah, Jazz," she sulked. Jazz could tell by the sound of her voice that something was wrong.

"Uh oh. What's going on?"

"Nothing. What's up?"

"Well, I have to get up with you soon, like really soon."

"Sure," she responded, attempting to rise up from the horrible mood she was headed down. "And by the way, I ended up getting the interview with Trina. Turns out she was only in for continued therapy. They kept her one night but let her go, despite the murder. She agreed to speak with me. The office assistant snagged the gig for me with her wit and charm and a couple of the dollars from my wallet. She has more skills networking than most of us do. She knows literally everyone, Jazz, like everyone."

"That's why your boss probably hired her, huh? But listen...this is very important. Meet me at my new location."

"So you really like it there so far?"

"I'm getting used to it, since my bosses bought them out, they made the transition over there easy. The office is only slightly smaller but the pay is bigger. Anyway, meet me downstairs, across the street at the deli at five o'clock. I'll be off by then and we can talk."

"Sounds serious, so I will try to get there by at least five-thirty. Oh wait...let me ask you about something that hit the news this morning."

"How about I'll see you when you get here?"

Charlotte was stomped by Jazz's abrupt interruption, but she simply agreed, hung up the phone and left to go interview Trina to hopefully get the recording she needed without taking things too far. It took forty-five minutes to reach her parent's home, and it was there where she spotted Trina already sitting outside on the wide porch.

As she drove up the large driveway to the house, a woman brought out a tray of what looked like drinks with a snack bowl in the center. The woman stroked Trina's hair before looking at Charlotte as she parked her car and exited. Then, she stood up behind Trina, causing Charlotte to assume that was her mother. Trying to appear as professional and as kind as she possibly could, Charlotte proceeded up the driveway, recorder already turned on in her small clutch and on her cell phone.

"Hello. My name is Charlotte Middleton..."

"The journalist. We are aware. Please come up and sit," the woman invited her. "I'm Trina's mother, and I know she doesn't need any permission of mine for this interview, but understand that if it gets out of hand at any point, she doesn't have to tell you to leave. I will. My home, my law." With that, the woman walked inside, leaving the door ajar, whispering her disgust about the interview loud enough so that they both could hear it.

"Don't worry about her. She's always like this when it comes to me."

"I hate that my presence bothers her so much. I really just want to ask some questions about, not so much what has been going on with you presently just yet, but..."

"My past. I remember what the other lady told me on the phone when we made this appointment."

"Good," Charlotte stated trying to lighten the tense mood with a broad smile. Trina hadn't smiled since she'd been in front of her. As a matter of fact, she remained straight faced and on guard, but Charlotte felt that most of the tension had to come from only days ago, losing a close friend and roommate, atop all the heartbreak of discovering her dead in the middle of traffic. "Will you tell me about Evans, your attacker, if you'd known him previously?"

"I don't know him. Stephen Evans. Never met him until that very day. He'd apparently followed me on social media, and from there found out where I lived to come and kill me…or preferably for him, those around me so that he could have me for himself. What else do you want to know? Do you want to know if there are two Stephen Evans? Seems like it to me." She finally turned her attention to the open yard. "Wherever I am, someone is murdered. I'm surprised they haven't locked me up in prison instead of a ward again."

There was a loose board that Trina started to kick, and each time she did, it made a soft thud against neighboring slabs of wood. She then turned back to Charlotte waiting on a question, however, the only response to her statement she got from the journalist's face was hesitation.

"Ask me. I want you to succeed, just like I want to succeed one day, so ask me. It's not your fault I'm in this mess."

Taking a deep breath, Charlotte decided to cut to the chase while she was still welcome at the house. It made no sense to ask questions to which she already knew the answers. The one question still remained.

"Would you like to know what happened to your husband Creed?" At the point the question bolted from her mouth, she could literally feel the heat travel up her spine and around her neck. The pain began to slither down her shoulders as the anxiety built, and when she saw Trina begin opening her mouth, she held her breath.

"Yes. Yes, I would like to know what that animal did to my husband. If he killed my child, I already know he killed Creed. To leave him out there…" she stated as a lone tear traveled down her cheek.

"I may be able to help you with that, Trina."

Just as fast as the tear fell from Trina's left eye, she wiped it away as she stood up and walked toward the front door that was left slightly open. Fearing that Trina was about to walk inside and never speak to her again, Charlotte stood up as well to go after her. However, once she saw Trina closing the door so that they could speak about the matter in more privacy, she quickly sat back down.

"Take a walk with me."

"Sure," Charlotte answered, removing her other tape recorder from her clutch so that it wouldn't catch the static of walking. She was willing to go almost anywhere Trina wanted to take her in order to get what she was there to get – her to speak to her stalker in an open way on the voice recorder. It was all or nothing, and hopefully, Evans kept his word.

"How do you suppose you can help me find Creed?"

"Evans."

She stopped in her tracks and turned to get eye to eye with Charlotte as they both stood at the end of the driveway. "Evans?"

"Yes. Let me be honest. I want to find out where Creed is as well because it's always been a puzzling yet rather fresh case that is still unsolved. The fact of the matter is that…"

"Evans knows."

"Exactly, and I spoke to him. He has conditions in which he will reveal where Creed is."

"And that has to do with me?"

"Yes. He wants you to basically tell him that you care for him and forgive him. He wants to hear your voice is what I gather."

"Don't gather. What exactly does he want?"

"He wants to talk to you...himself," she paused. "I figured that the only way would be via recorder, and I would play it for him."

"Don't ever figure. I'll go to him. I'll go to him with you. You get the exclusive and then we will find out where Creed is. A win win." Trina's face was stoic. "We will both get what is of vital importance to us."

"Thank you...thank you so much," Charlotte responded awkwardly.

"No. There's no need to thank me. Let's just get this done. This is between you and me only," she stated quickly looking at her parent's house and back at Charlotte. "Make the date, and give me a call. I promise to be available."

"Will do. Will do, Trina." Charlotte walked back to her car, satisfied with the interview, but afraid to show how excited she actually was while backing out of the driveway as Trina watched. Checking her rear, she pulled completely out, and as she turned to face Trina again, she'd already moved to the front of Charlotte's car, startling her. After a half nod Trina's way, she started driving down the road while in her side mirror, she watched Trina's mother walk onto the porch.

She let out a deep breath, excited as ever, so elated that she then decided to drive directly to Dr. Cranizi's office.

It was her day off, and if she could lock this exclusive meeting in with Stephen Evans and Trina as soon as possible, it was as good as a promotion either at her job or somewhere else. That was all she needed to break free from her old life and from needing to lean on Tyrese any longer. His cheating ways had finally caused her to make up her mind, something she should have done a while ago.

**

"Dr. Cranizi. I don't have an appointment," she stated as the guard looked through what Charlotte assumed was a list of appointments. "I just need to see him…"

"Your name, please."

"Charlotte Middleton."

She looked toward the building as she listened to him radio something back beyond the gate. Starting to get nervous, she wondered if it was safe with all the extra precautions that were being done, unlike her last visit.

"Excuse me. Is everything alright in there?"

The guard raised his hand and gave her the thumbs up as he allowed her through. "Just had to be certain the ward was completely secure and patients off the yard first."

"Which ward was that?"

"The one you're headed to…without an appointment. Next time, make one. There's an event out here just about every week that doesn't make the news," he said looking at the badge hanging from her neck. "Hardly enough staff. Take that off."

"Oh…I…sorry," she stumbled as she drove through, making her way to the same building as before. She didn't even have to go inside the building to see Dr. Cranizi as he was stepping outside of a car as she pulled up.

"Dr. Cranizi, may I have a word with you? It will only take a second of your time."

"A second's wasting," he stated as he continued to walk, causing Charlotte to throw her car in gear and chase him down.

"May I have one more appointment with your patient, Stephen Evans, as soon as possible?"

"And when would you like that appointment set up."

"Could we make it...anytime that is feasible for you...and him for that matter," she continued to speak, yet frustrated with the way she felt like she was talking to the back of his feet. Therefore, she stopped walking and said the one thing she knew would get his attention. "Trina. The young lady who he stalked. She wants to speak with him as soon as possible."

Just like Charlotte thought, Dr. Cranizi stopped dead in his tracks.

**

Jazz sat at the deli across the street from her job, not really paying attention to much at all. Even though it was already five-thirty and the traffic was bumper to bumper, Charlotte had never stood her up before, and she highly doubted she would do it this time. She tapped on the wrought iron table nervously as she slumped over to hold her head in her hand. Droplets of water began to take over her vision as she thought about remaining silent about what she knew could end her friendship. She'd never held on to something of this magnitude, and it almost made her want to vomit just knowing that she had to tell this to her best friend.

As she sulked there at the table that sat within the fenced barrier of the deli, she noticed Charlotte's car pull into the parking garage where she worked. She took a deep breath as she pulled out her make-up case and fiddled with the mirror in order to check her eyes. They'd been friends for so long until the slightest hint of betrayal would be evident long before she uttered a word.

"Here goes nothing," she whispered to herself as she created the absolute best smile she could muster while Charlotte ran across the street.

"Hey…oh! Don't you really look like your brand new self today! New make-up?"

"Oh stop playing. You know I hated that shade of brown foundation on my face. It didn't quite match, but this one really looks like my Nubian-ness, neck and all. I don't have to blend it in with another shade."

"Well, I like it," she squealed, tossing her string, blonde hair up into a ponytail, ready to relax and eat. "I see you got me my favorite," she said referring to the small sandwich Jazz had waiting for her at the table. She reached into her pocket and pulled out a ten dollar bill, sliding it across the table. "There ya' go."

"Girl, stop. It isn't even about that…this time. You treated me last time, remember?" she laughed. "So how are things going with you and Tyrese. Last time we talked, you were getting the third degree about interviewing that madman."

"We're not good right now…but I don't want to ruin the rest of my night after I have some great news to tell you, but you can't tell a soul and I mean like nobody…"

"Well, wait though, C." Jazz placed her sweet tea down and inhaled as she sat all the way back in her chair. Then she stared at Charlotte like she was about to lose her only friend whom she loved like a sister.

"What is it, Jazz?"

"It's about Tyrese."

"What about him?"

"Remember that night I told you I had to be to work, a couple nights ago, the same day you interviewed that stalker guy? As I was pulling in," she paused and looked back at the parking garage, "I believe I saw Tyrese pulling out."

"Say what now?"

Jazz's voice started to shake, so she swallowed and calmed herself before she continued, "I was going to tell you sooner, but…"

"But what, Jazz? You mean you caught him at the damn hotel and you're just now telling me about it? So what, he had a woman with him?"

"No, no he didn't, but his car was leaning to the side, like he had a busted tire, as he drove out." Her voice quieted. "I looked right at him. I knew it was him. Our eyes met. He looked startled to see me, I guess because you didn't tell him about my transfer."

"No, no I didn't, Jazz," Charlotte looked at her in disbelief, and all Jazz could do was stare back at her expressionless because there was more. She just didn't know how to say it. As Charlotte sat there stunned at how Jazz kept the fact that her husband was at a hotel, possibly with some woman, the one thing that stood out about the story was the flat tire. Tyrese had told her that he got the flat as he drove to the drug store. "What do you mean his car was leaning?"

"It was a flat tire, C, as he left the hotel's garage. I looked. There's more though."

"Well damn, Jazz!"

"There was a woman found in a hotel room. She'd been cut all over, cut open. She was sitting in the bathtub, and she'd been waiting for someone to show up. I recognized Tyrese on one of the cameras we watched."

"What do you mean you recognized Tyrese? Exactly what are you saying?" Charlotte's eyes pierced through Jazz like a stack of sharpened knives, and Jazz's stomach turned sour as she didn't know how else to say what was coming next.

"Charlotte," she started, reaching for her hand, but Charlotte snatched her hand back. Jazz started to cry, but Charlotte didn't budge.

"He was coming out of the room. I didn't see his face, but when I reviewed the tape with everyone else, I knew it was him. His head was down. He went in, and it wasn't long before he came back out. I didn't tell. I didn't tell anyone that I knew who it was, and I won't unless you give me the word."

Charlotte didn't say a word. She thought back to earlier when they both watched the news and how he stood there like he was about to pass out before slamming his fist into the wall. It was that same news report that threw him into that rage, and the whole time, she thought it was her questioning him.

"I have to leave, Jazz." Without another word, Charlotte got up, leaving her good friend there to chase behind her. When Jazz grabbed her arm, Charlotte swung her arm around with tears flowing down her face.

"Get off of me! There's no way, Jazz! None! You know it. He could never in his life…he's a lot of things I don't like, but I would never fall in love with someone who could do that. Ever! And you shouldn't have kept this from me!" Charlotte fell into what Jazz saw as a state of denial which was what she feared. She knew the information would damage her friendship if Charlotte sided with Tyrese.

"Please, Charlotte, just listen to me!" she yelled back at her best friend as she watched her tangle with traffic to get across the busy street. What she didn't realize was that Charlotte did believe her, but she just couldn't accept it. It all made sense.

When she got home, she raced through an empty house. Tyrese was nowhere in sight, and that was both good for her and him. As she packed a light bag with her laptop, change of clothes for work and some workout clothes, she already decided that she didn't want to see him for at least twenty-four hours. She had too much on her plate, and he obviously had too much on his. He hadn't even called her all day, and since she gathered the news about his liaison from Jazz, her heart simply couldn't bear it, toppled with the fact that he was spotted at a murder scene.

"I can't deal with this," she cried uncontrollably until she finally stopped to look at her reflection. She came from a heroin addicted mother who tossed her on the side of the road and a thief for a father who'd much rather adore her from a crack in the bathroom door as she washed than read her a story while she was fully clothed. "I can do this," she reaffirmed. "I can, and I will. I've done it before with nothing, and I'll do it again." She shoved some socks into her bag and just as she was about to put it over her shoulder, she threw it against the wall as hard as she could. "Dammit! Damn you, Tyrese!" Then she looked around at her bedroom, snatched up the bag, and left. "Time for me to get my shit together. All or nothing."

She didn't stop driving until she was only a couple minutes away from her place of employment. Only two blocks away from her job was a swanky hotel that she felt she deserved to treat herself to for one night. In order to motivate herself in life, she always felt she needed two things along with a great prayer to God, and those two things were daily goals that had to be attained and ways to treat herself better than anyone in her life ever could. She would order directly from their menu for dinner and remain focused on the one goal she'd had since the news broke of Trina once again – finding Creed. The bit of information that she wasn't able to let Jazz in on was that she'd already planned the meet up with Stephen Evans and Trina. It was to be done at three o'clock next week on Monday, and nothing, not even Tyrese, Jazz or a dead woman in a tub would stop her. In the meantime, she turned off her cell phone and started to defy the life that she knew wasn't meant for her for a better one. It wasn't long before that she decided to send a text to Jazz, apologizing for walking off over something so honest while at the same time letting her know where she was and to meet her at the gym on the second floor later to work some aggression off.

**

"Where are you? Where are you, baby, come on," he continued to search after picking up his car from being fixed. He pressed her number once again, but as it went on to the third ring, he knew that she wasn't going to pick it up. All he knew was that he didn't want to lose his marriage behind anything, including his cheating ways. It was this time, however, that he'd finally gathered up the courage to tell Charlotte all about what happened and didn't happen the other night. He didn't know when or if things would take a turn down the wrong path, but it was a path he was desperately trying not to go down.

With a new set of wheels on the front of his luxury automobile, he turned at the next light in order to pass Charlotte's job. Sometimes she ended up working late, especially when they were arguing about anything, so the only place she could have possibly been was there, Tyrese thought to himself as he circled the block. However, as he drove around multiple times, her car was nowhere to be found. Then, his cell phone rang, and he rushed to answer without even looking at the caller's identification.

"Hello? Hello?"

"Tyrese?"

"Yeah, who is this? Is this Jazz?" he asked confused because it was extremely rare for her to call his cell phone unless absolutely necessary.

"Yeah, it's me, Ty. Is Charlotte around? I've been calling, and she hasn't picked up at all," she asked, not going into detail about much because she didn't know how much he had already been informed about. As she waited on him to respond, she prepared herself for the worst.

"I was just looking for her, Jazz. I hadn't seen her since this morning nor talked to her. Have you?"

Jazz said nothing as she listened to his panicked breathing through the phone. She imagined the man who was on the other end behaving like a panicked animal, but then she snapped out of her daze in disbelief.

"Hello? Jazz?"

"Yeah, I'm here. Dead area. What was that now?"

"I said I haven't seen her. How about you?"

"I spoke to her earlier, but since then, nothing."

"How much earlier?"

"Around five thirty actually."

"On the phone or what? Because I hadn't seen her or spoken to her."

"We spoke face to face…in front of my job. Well, across the street from it," she fumbled then finally said it, "Keystone Hotel." Her throat quivered like she had a knife to her throat, and it was Tyrese holding the knife at the handle. What she couldn't see was Tyrese, however. His hand started to shake at the wheel, and he pulled over into a park on the side of the road.

"Keystone," he repeated back to her. The air conditioning was on full blast in the car, but he began to sweat like he was in the middle of a desert. His mouth went numb while his throat quivered as he spoke the words aloud again. "Keystone Hotel. That *was* you. I did see you." There was a pause. "When did you start working there?" he stated, trying to sound normal.

"My people bought out their people. I went in on a transfer to train and manage, you know, the same job with a few extra perks." She stopped talking momentarily. "Were you meeting someone or did you have…"

"A meeting. Work related. But uhh…I heard something happened out there on the news this morning. Something like…"

"A murder," she answered. "A bloody murder." His breathing sent pains through her ear as she waited on his response.

"Yeah, that…I suppose that was what you and Charlotte were meeting about then being that she wants to get a big story like that somehow?"

Jazz didn't say a word when a text message came through on her phone. She kept the phone to her ear for about fifteen seconds as she waited on him to interrupt her silence. Then she finally said it, and it rang like fire in Tyrese's ears. "You did it, didn't you?" There was no follow up to her statement, and she continued. "I saw you…on tape."

"It wasn't me." Shaken with fear and controlled totally by his reflexes, he ended the call and sped off. "It wasn't me!" he hollered, turning the music on full blast in attempts to drown out his life. As he drove erratically down the road, suffering from sheer panic out of believing Charlotte was doing one thing…planning to leave him. Then, he would be all on his own.

There was no stopping him from racing to his house. Everything was quiet on his street, and it was his car that made the most noise as it hurled itself into the driveway, nearly nabbing the garage with the front of his car. Rushing from the car, he bolted through the door and immediately began searching for any and everything he needed to get out of town.

There was a stash of money that he kept in the pantry of the kitchen that he even hid from Charlotte. It was in plain sight which he'd learned was the best way to conceal a thing. He reached inside the hole, and there it was – all five-thousand dollars. Rushing to get out of town, he moved through the kitchen to grab as many snacks as he could pack into a plastic bag so he wouldn't have to stop anywhere that could get him on video. The only comfort he stood in was that Charlotte was his wife, and if she cared at all for him, she would call him soon and never turn him in because she would never be forced to do so, especially for something that only looks like he may have done.

As he was just about to run down the hallway, that was when he heard it, a sound that made his heart leap from his chest. It was the shower. He grabbed the wall and exhaled, exhausted from having had to deal with the situation all alone. He needed Charlotte. He needed her just to keep his sanity.

"Baby, baby," he called out for her as he drifted toward the bathroom door, becoming increasingly comforted by the presence of the woman he'd betrayed so much. "Charlotte, baby," he continued as he turned the knob on the bathroom door. It was open as usual, and he walked inside with his head down, overly sensitive to the moisture that felt like a secure blanket covering his vulnerable skin. "Hey, uh, baby," he stammered as he leaned against the counter, holding back tears. "I think I messed up, really bad and uh…somebody is trying to set me up for something that I didn't do. I'm sorry for the way I acted," he stated as he looked a bit closer to the shower and noticed the sound of the water never changed. "Charlotte?"

Slowly, he moved toward the shower curtain, and when he didn't see as much as a thin outline of a shadow, his pulse began to race as thoughts of Patrice lying dead in the hotel tub took over. Terrified that it could also be Charlotte, he yanked the shower curtain back so hard it ripped from the shower pole like nothing held it there but thin thread. The shower curtain dropped from his hand, and when he saw no one inside the tub, the brawny man went limp and at once, fell forward to only catch himself on the edge of the tub. Exhaustion ruled over him as he hadn't eaten much for a couple days nor had he had the mindset to work-out, however, the relief he felt that Charlotte hadn't met the same fate as Patrice, took its toll, and he had to lie down.

Figuring Charlotte hadn't gotten into the shower yet, he made his way into the bedroom, panting as if he was on his last breath. By the time he got to the hallway, the walls were spinning, and as he turned to the left, for a split second, he thought he saw someone staring at him from the opposite direction – in the direction of the living room.

"Charlotte?" he called. "Talk to me, please. I need your help. Not feeling too good right now. I'm sorry. I know Jazz probably told you..." he continued as he stumbled back down toward the living area. Before he made it to the end of the hall, he heard a drawer close in the kitchen.

"Told her what?" a voice asked.

Tyrese ducked like someone took a swing at him but there was no one there. Stumbling backwards against the wall, he started backing up until he could get himself together. He made a move into the bedroom and planted himself behind the door to make his head stop spinning. After a couple of seconds went by, he was able to stand with a clearer head and clenched his fists to defend himself against whoever it was in the house.

"Who the hell is that?" he shouted in the boldest and most fearless voice that he could. When he got no answer, he made his way down the hallway slowly. "I said who the hell is there? Charlotte, stop playin'!" Even though he was weakened, he knew he was much stronger than most women he'd ever known, so he was prepared to take whoever it was down. "This is not the time!" he shouted once again, until he heard a car door slam from the front of his yard, followed by the sound of an engine and a car leaving.

Bolting from the hallway, he ran into the kitchen where he left his stash of money and car keys. They were no longer there. "Dammit!" The only thing he saw that he missed before somehow was a note that read *I'll be back. I'm at The Summits. Need to clear my head.*

"What? Who the hell was just in my damn house?" he asked himself as he picked up the note and ran to the front door to only find out that the intruder left with his car. "The fuck?" Still confused, he shouted after the car believing that it truly could have been Charlotte. "Charlotte! Man, shit!" he yelled frustrated, walking back into the house and slamming the door. He walked to the refrigerator, took out the half gallon of orange juice and took it down in an attempt to end his dizziness. Feeling like he was losing his mind, he sat down at the table and read the note over and over again. Then, he placed his full concentration back on the front door, and then he noticed. He quickly turned to notice that the back door wasn't locked, but when he ran to the front door, it was. He'd had to open it when he never heard the noisy lock turn.

"What the...?" His mind and heart began to race as he ran only five steps to the garage door and yanked it open. His emotions sank down to his feet. Charlotte's car - it wasn't there. It really was an intruder. "Fuck!" He raced to the kitchen table again, totally forgetful of the fact that the car keys were no longer there as well as the cash. Therefore, he pulled his wallet from his back pocket and his cell phone from his side and began to dial. Before the person on the other end completed the greeting, Tyrese belted out, "I need a cab fast."

**

Changing clothes felt like a nightmare for Charlotte. Just like when she was a child, the only thing she wanted to do was disappear or remain asleep whenever the bad things in her life would go worse. However, she'd learned better, and the best thing for her was to keep going with her days and nights as usual, throughout all the heartache, and accept tragedy just as it came without allowing it to take her own life away.

Sliding on her sneakers, tears began to flow down her face, and as she tied her laces, she began to encourage herself aloud, "Just keep things going. You were a woman before him. You were a journalist before him. You have overcome many obstacles before him. Love will come again. Just keep living. No apologies. No apologies, Charlotte."

She stood up from the chair, did a light jog and stretch in the room as she stared at herself in the mirror, mentally preparing herself to meet with Jazz and not completely break down. Then, she headed out the door. As she headed down the corridor, she decided to shut her eyes for about three seconds during her stroll. She used those seconds to refocus her energy into keeping herself healthy and fit. When she opened them again, she felt ready for anything, and a peace came over her that she'd missed out on since she met with Jazz. Finally, she smiled again on the inside.

"Things are going to be just fine," she whispered as she hit the elevator button. It opened right away, and she entered only to press the number two. She watched as the elevator doors closed and thought about the chapter of her life that she would be closing while opening another in just one week with Evans and Trina.

"This is the kind of stuff that paves the way for anyone successful. My success…finally. Something that *I* will control in my life." The elevator stopped, and she got off. It wasn't surprising at all that the gym was completely empty when she arrived. She'd never stayed in any hotel where the gym was jam packed, but for tonight, an empty gym was just what she needed. Figuring she'd start at the treadmill, she jumped on. It wasn't long before she was startled by Jazz sneaking up beside her and running along on the adjacent treadmill.

"Hey, girl," Jazz spoke without looking her way as she started the treadmill up.

"Well hi there, Jazz. Sneak up on me, why don't you?" Charlotte grinned as her feet continued to hit the running area.

"You know how I am. Move like a tiger, but fast like a cheetah. So look, I'm sorry about everything…"

"Don't be. You're in love, right? No matter what he did or does, there's nothing wrong with being in love. Just go with it. I thought about it. Even if he did do it," she said, stopping the treadmill in order to walk behind Charlotte to the weight bench where she noticed her cell phone on the floor. "He did it to her, not to you. He would never do that to you which proves he loves you."

Charlotte didn't answer but only slowed her jog to a fast gait, confused at what Jazz was saying. "What are you talking about? If he did what you are insinuating he did then are you saying that he had a right to kill her? Is that what you're saying?" she asked as she lowered the elevation and stared at the white wall directly in front of her. Jazz never answered, and when seconds went by, a frustrated Charlotte turned off the exercise equipment and turned to face Jazz. "What are you saying, Jazz? Jazz?" She was nowhere in the room.

"Charlotte, I'm back here," she heard her call from around the corner. There was a section that led to a small pool and locker room around the corner. "This is nice back here. And yeah, I thought about it. If anyone should die, it's the other woman in the life of the man you love."

"Jazz," Charlotte called as she walked away from the treadmill and suspiciously walked in the direction of Jazz's voice, wondering why she abruptly walked away. Everything was quiet and even when she thought she heard something behind her, she looked backwards, and there was nothing. Therefore, she decided to speak again. "Jazz are you alright back here?"

She approached the wall that would take her just around the corner from the weights and called her name again before finally walking around the dimly lit corner, "Jazz?" As the total scope of the room came into focus, there was no sign of Jazz. "Really, Jazz? This is just like you," she stated as she walked over by the miniature pool. "I forgive you already, so come out come out wherever you are," she sang as she turned back around on her tip toes to go back into the weight room area. "Because I'm going back into the weight room." As she stepped away from the pool, something grabbed her ankle and pulled with excessive force, plummeting her to the hard floor face forward. Her face ricocheted off the floor and blood scattered across the floor from her nose as she was pulled into the water. Suffocating on her own blood and shock, she scrambled to catch her grip on the slippery floor while gasping for air, but nothing worked as she sank into the small, yet deep pool of water, only to be thrown around and choked by the hands of her friend Jazz.

Her hands slammed against the water as Jazz held her by the throat with a death grip. She was completely naked as she toyed with Charlotte's life, enjoying the torment she placed on her.

"You forgive me now? There was one other thing that I forgot to tell you, Charlotte. He said he would leave you. He told me that he loved me, and that he loved me very much," she stated as the force of her hands squeezed the life from Charlotte's bloody face. Charlotte continued to fight, but fighting Jazz was like fighting a brick wall. She wasn't budging.

Jazz began to grin as she shoved Charlotte's head back and forth hoping she died quickly. "You always would tell me he was a liar. I found that out myself." Before Charlotte's head fell lifeless, she said one more thing, "Tyrese cheated on me, too."

Charlotte's eyes and body went into total distress, her eyes glaring back at Jazz with a pain she'd never felt before in her life, and as she gave the woman she knew as her friend one last hit to try and get away, her head went limp. Jazz loosened her grip just slightly, stuck her hand into Charlotte's pockets until she felt the room key, and then, allowed her to fall into the water slowly as she removed herself from the pool. She walked over to the clothing she'd tossed behind a stack of chairs no more than ten feet away from the scene of Charlotte's death, got dressed and then walked away. When she returned to the weight room, she retrieved Charlotte's cell phone and sent a text message.

**

He stared down at his phone as he stood impatiently on the porch, pacing back and forth, heavily concerned about the wife he'd done so wrong over the years. Unable to keep still, he continued to move, swinging his arms as if he needed to hold on to something and leaning over the porch rail until a vibration jolted him to a standstill. Nearly dropping the phone from nervousness, he answered it on the first vibration, but there was no voice on the other end.

"Hello? Hello?" he repeated but pulled the phone from his ear to see a text message. It was from Charlotte. Fumbling to open the message, he finally got it open, and it read, "I'm in Room 652. I want to see you. I have something to talk to you about."

Immediately after he read it, he began typing a message back, questioning her about if she had come home and if she has her car or even his car? He even explained that he had to take a cab and for her to wait on him and to keep the doors locked because someone was setting him up. As he typed, he waited on a response, but he got none. Then, the cab came driving down the street. With only his wallet and cell phone along with the only money he had on him at the time, he left, hoping that the taxi could take him all the way there. Unfortunately, as he watched the meter turn down street after street for about ten minutes, he knew he was going to have to stop the cab and finish the rest of the way on foot.

"Thanks," he stated, hopping out of the taxi after giving him all the money he had left on him. The Summits Hotel was still a hefty distance away, about seven blocks, but he had to make it there as fast as he could. As soon as he shut the cab's door, he started running. There weren't as many people on the streets as he thought there would be, so there was hardly anything slowing him down. Darting in front of cars and jumping out of their way was the only option as he knew for a fact that Charlotte's life was in danger although he didn't quite know how or by whom. All he knew was that it had to do with him, and he desperately needed her to do whatever it took to stay away from anyone she didn't know or to whom she wasn't familiar.

Stopping in front of a closed newspaper stand, he began to text his wife again because since he'd left their home, there hadn't been a return text.

"Come on, Charlotte, come on!" He searched the streets just to see if he could get there safely by using a short cut, but he didn't know the area well enough to chance it. Therefore, he kept running at full speed until he ran the next two blocks that brought him to the entrance of the hotel. As soon as he ran through the doors, the stairs were his next option because waiting on the elevator with four others that were already there was bound to slow him up. Completely exhausted from running full throttle to the hotel, he struggled to leap up the staircase, heaving with each level he approached until he finally fell against the door at the sixth level.

Tyrese's chest felt like it could cave in from the power of his lungs expanding in his chest. He felt he'd pushed himself far too hard while running and couldn't catch his breath.

"Charlotte," he gasped as he leaned onto the door handle causing the door to open. He then struggled down the hallway reading the numbers on each door and realized that Room 652 was more toward the other end of the corridor. Therefore, he continued walking, each step bringing less exhaustion, until he stood at the room door. The key was stuck inside the lock, and Tyrese didn't hesitate opening the door.

"Charlotte!" he shouted, closing the door behind himself, ready to get her to some sort of safety. He was confused, but he'd chosen to only focus on the concrete things he knew – his wife and his love for her. Anything else became secondary to him for the very first time in his life, and he just wanted her to be okay.

He was led into the room, and it was set up just like the other hotel room was causing him to stumble against a chair and stare in disbelief. There was a champagne bottle with a note hanging from it identical to the other note, and written in the color red were the words *I'll never leave you lonely, Tyrese.* Tyrese's legs lost all strength as he dropped into the chair that was located directly behind him, turning his attention from the neatly folded back bed to the closed bathroom door.

"Oh God," he cried. "No, no, not Charlotte…not my baby. No," he cried, falling to his knees and crawling to the bathroom door like a six month old child. The door didn't shove open, so he turned the knob as he body tensed into knots. His entire body shook from fear as his hand fell hard against the floor and his eyes stared hopelessly at the pulled shower curtain. "My baby," he cried. "I'm so sorry, so so sorry. This wasn't supposed to happen. I don't know what's going on!" he shouted as he slammed his fist into the bathroom cabinet, and it was in the next second that Tyrese ripped the shower curtain completely down from the pole. There was no Charlotte, just a tub full of water.

Jumping up from the floor, Tyrese hit the water with his fists, infuriated that someone was toying with his head and playing games that he didn't want to play. Suddenly, his cell phone vibrated. He knew it was a text message, so he took it from his pocket. It read *I'm in the gym on the second floor whenever you make it here.*

All the fear seemed to have disappeared from Tyrese's demeanor as he stormed through the bathroom door and headed straight for the gym. Tyrese had tunnel vision, and he behaved like a lion raging through the jungle as he'd already sensed that it wasn't his wife texting him from the phone. His veins seemed to rip apart his skin as they pulsated violently at his temples, and as he made it to the second floor, he followed the sign that led to the direction of the gym. As soon as he got there, there was a paper sign that read *closed for repair* taped to the glass on the door, but the door was ajar. He looked inside. When he saw no one, he went in anyway, closing the door behind him and prepared for war with the unknown.

The gym was quiet, but Tyrese was more cautious than he'd ever been in his entire life. There were too many variables that he had to take into account in one area, and one wrong move could get him killed. He knew that he was engaging with a psychopath, so instead of calling for Charlotte, he called for the unknown person he knew was trying to set him up for murder.

"Where's Charlotte? Who are you?" he demanded, searching the room, hoping for an answer. His hopes were rewarded.

"Does it matter? And that's the answer to both your questions." The voice came from another area of the gym, and there was enough echo to confuse Tyrese as he didn't know there was another area with a pool.

"Who are you?" he asked, lifting a twenty pound barbell from the floor as his weapon of choice.

"So soon we forget. But I saw you in the hotel, Tyrese. You lied to me," she stated calmly, and it was only then that he realized who it was by the sound of her voice.

"Jazz?"

"In the flesh...or is that all you loved about me?"

Tyrese stared back at her in horror as he recounted his affair with his wife's best friend. That was when he knew. He knew it was her as she stood there with the one thing that linked her to Charlotte's whereabouts – the cell phone. He'd been set up.

"What the fuck did you do?" Then he shouted. "Where's my wife?"

Jazz just stood there, silently elated about what she'd done all in the name of causing him heartache through revenge.

**

"Can you take over for me? I really have to go to the bathroom bad. It's an emergency like no other. Here are my keys. Please. I'll be right back."

"Okay, no problem. Just hurry back." She looked around her, slightly lost at the front desk but stood there confidently as a young lady walked toward her. "It's a wonderful day here at Keystone. Do you have a reservation?" she spoke cheerfully to the lady who was smiling as she observed the lobby.

"No, however, I need to get a really romantic room for a man I'm trying to impress."

"Really?" she stated, grinning as the young lady was so forthcoming which wasn't something she was accustomed to, especially since she hardly ever worked the front desk. However, to show that she was paying attention, she decided to encourage the female's liaison. "Must be a great young man."

"Well, it's a surprise, and he is great. He doesn't know that I'm into him like that, but I've been watching him for a while, and I can tell this high dollar engineer has been checking for me, too. His reputation is under wraps but I unwrapped it. He's a pretty easy take down, just hard to keep taken. I worked with him before so I know his ways, but you know how it is when you're not put together to get attention in the beginning," she laughed, tapping the bottom of her breasts, eluding to the fact that she got work done in the most attention gathering places on her body as to attract a man. "He never knew I existed, but now, I am definitely his speed."

"An engineer, huh? I know a couple, and if you can snag him, then you have yourself a winner. How many nights?"

"Two please, and here is my identification and credit card. His name is Tyrese, and girl, he's mine after tonight," she stated, tossing his name out there so that she could gauge if the hotel representative knew him. However, when the representative said nothing, she continued. "Once I put it on him, he'll never want that wife again, girlfriend. I need a man, so I've got to take what I can get. You're single, you understand, right?" she asked, obviously very aggressive and sure of herself while unashamed of anything she stated.

The stand in receptionist looked down at her left hand's ring finger, and just before she answered, she heard someone calling her name.

"Thanks, Mrs. Jazz. You're a life saver. My relief didn't come in to work, so it's just me handling all this. Will you see if you can get someone here to cover me for lunch? Mrs. Jazz?"

"Oh...sure," she stuttered, then turned back to the new patron. "Let me finish up here, and I need you to sign here and here for me. And here is your room key...429."

"Thanks. If I see you later on tonight, I'll let you know. And may I have a second key, please?" she winked.

"Sure," Jazz answered, winking back as if she was amused, but inside, she was torn to shreds. Immediately, she left the building to go sit inside her car as a whole hour and a half went by. The more she thought about the young lady whose name she learned was Patrice, the more she saw the man she'd fallen in love with lying with her all night long. Her relationship with him had already grown more complicated than any other relationship that she'd known. He was supposed to be in love with her, in love enough to leave his wife...her friend...eventually. She was supposed to be the only other woman in his life.

She thought about the last time they'd met up at the hotel she transferred from. Whenever Charlotte worked late, he would come automatically. They never called one another ever. Jazz always knew Charlotte's schedule being her best friend and Tyrese did as well, so it was easy to know when to meet up and when to depart. Their last time together was one month ago. They'd decided to stop until things could be shut down in a way that Charlotte could be hurt the least. Until that time, they were supposed to go on as usual, and he'd promised her that he only loved her and wanted no other woman, although she was the other woman.

Her phone rang. It was Charlotte. She wiped her eyes, calmed herself down, and answered. "Hello?"

"This is boring as hell, Jazz," Charlotte complained as she sat in a seat as far to the back as she could get, holding her pen in one hand with her pad on her lap and tablet in the other hand while she spoke through her cell phone's ear piece.

"It could be worse. You could be working from home like me, hoping to get out and do something productive. Girl, I can barely move in here without taking some pain killers…and that only gives me relief for a couple hours until I have to pop another one. Top it off, later I have to go in to work to pick something up, and then it will be right back home for me."

"What are you working on?"

"Some of this and that. How about you? What's this event all about you're on?"

"It's this grand opening of the former governor's. You know, that big secret she'd proclaimed she would have in a couple years. Well, here it is…a restaurant. You'll read all about it with my name drowned out in the boredom of the whole article."

"Be quiet, Charlotte," Jazz giggled at her friend sounding so glum about her gig. "You are an excellent writer, and I'm sure you'll find something at the event to bring it to life. I'm willing to bet on it."

"Listen, Jazz, I'll talk to you later. Gotta go."

"Bye…Charlotte." She listened to the call go silent, and she stared out of her car window as she repeated in a low, dismal tone. "Bye, Charlotte." It was then that she waited and watched the entire day, overcome with heartache and jealousy as she continuously replayed the conversation she had with Patrice at the counter. She began to weep silently as she started up her car and moved it to another location. From there, she waited, having already decided that she would be in her office later for what she'd already planned on doing that night.

Jazz entered Room 429 as she watched the woman in question leave the hotel's premises. From there, she entered with her own master key, and it was there she remained until Patrice got back. Those at the hotel figured she'd gone to work at home until that night, and that was the story she'd stuck to with everyone – that she felt ill. It was the easiest lie to tell being that she'd come back inside Keystone Hotel through the back after moving her car away from the hotel.

While inside, she digested what would happen that night, how she would be betrayed by the man she loved. She wanted to repay him with something he would never forget while the tears drenched her face as she stood over what she knew would be their love bed. Even though she didn't know for certain that Tyrese would show up, she felt quite certain he would. What man wouldn't? Besides, he slept with her, and she was his wife's best friend. He was going to show up, and Jazz was sure of it.

As she stood there, she pulled out a brand new knife she'd purchased from the store. It was her best purchase of the day, and she'd just got it from a store down the street before returning to the hotel. She wrapped it up and held it inside her blazer that she wore over some jeans. From there, she waited in the connecting, empty hotel room for any sound that Patrice was excited, expecting him, and all alone. It wasn't long before Patrice came through the door, singing her heart out, and on the phone with someone gloating about her night.

"No, girl. All I can tell you is that I've practically stalked this man since I've known him, and now that I'm fit and fine, he doesn't even realize I'm the same girl from back in the day that he never, ever looked at. Whatever though, because he should be on his way. He assured me of that at the office in more than one way. Look, lemme call you after this whole deal. When I want something, what happens? And stop asking me who it is! I'll tell you after I get my photo as proof. You're gonna be shocked." She boasted, bursting out laughing at the answer someone gave her on the other end of the phone, and as soon as they were finished talking, she ended the call and tossed the phone in her purse.

Jazz tightened the knife in her hand as her throat trembled, not from fear, but a magnitude of envy and anger that she'd never felt before in her life. She thought about all Tyrese promised her as well as how she put her friendship at risk for what she wanted more than anything in the world – love. She really loved Tyrese, so much to a point that she began to believe that the only reason he dipped out on Charlotte was because she wasn't his true love. It was the same reason he told her.

A door shut in Patrice's hotel room, and Jazz listened hard. The water in the tub came on, and after waiting for about five minutes with no other sounds coming from the room, she entered. There was lingerie on the floor, and even a bottle of champagne on ice. Jazz walked directly in front of the bathroom door and listened to Patrice hum a song. It sounded like she was in the bathtub already, so she opened the door quickly and shut it behind her. Patrice's head lifted up from the water's edge and as her hand slid down the side of the shower curtain to pull it back, Jazz attacked.

Shoving Patrice's head down in the water along with her body, she shoved the knife through her belly and up toward her chest and the rest was left in blood on the bathtub's walls and water. No one heard a thing as the water suffocated all the sound. She slipped through the adjoining hotel room door after it was all done, cleaned herself up in the room, and then, hid the bloody knife back in the same plastic bag beneath her blazer that she'd worn inside. She'd even written a small note on the card that hung from the champagne bottle that the woman she'd murdered hadn't had the opportunity to fill out yet, along with another notice inside the tub with a bloody Patrice.

Jazz walked. She calmly walked all the way to the other end of the hallway, beyond the elevators. This was where her waiting began. Soon, she saw just who she was waiting on walking onto the fourth floor from the staircase. Her cell phone was already on, and she hit record. She caught his every movement before he entered the room. Then, she fled the fourth floor, taking the same stairs he entered from so that she could find his car in the parking garage.

Carefully, she walked around the cameras until she could dispose of the bloody knife in the one place she knew would link him to the murder – his tire – because if she couldn't have him all to herself, she believed that he shouldn't have been available for anyone else. Then, she walked back to her own car, prepared to drive into the parking garage to go to her office as if she'd done nothing at all.

** **

"What did *I* do to Charlotte? I simply told her that you killed that girl at Keystone. Don't act like you didn't look me in my face when I pulled into that parking garage. You looked right at me…and you should know my face from anywhere, even in the pitch black of night." Jazz's appearance was ice cold as she spoke to Tyrese, a demeanor that he'd never seen before.

"I didn't kill anyone, Jazz. That's not even me."

"Well, she can't talk to you right now, so that's why I have the phone. But, you tell me something. Why the hell did you walk into her hotel room at about nine o'clock...like you did on this video?" She lifted up her cell phone and showed him a moving image that he could barely make out from where he stood. "I must admit to this one... I lied when I said the hotel camera caught you coming out of the room. No hotel camera caught you. I already knew that the fourth floor corridor's cameras were out, and Ms. Patrice didn't know what was coming for her when she took the key right from my hand."

Tyrese stared back at her as he began to lower the dumbbell. Patrice noticed his surrender and continued.

"Yeah, I gave her the perfect key...the perfect wounds...and the perfect alibi." She hit the emergency button on her phone, and it picked up before Tyrese even knew what was happening. "Help!" she screamed before sprinting to the other side of the gym. "He's trying to kill me! Help me, please! Tyrese!"

"Jazz," he called out before he bolted for the phone, but she'd already darted to the other side of the gym where Charlotte floated inside the pool. As soon as he turned the corner behind Jazz, she'd run to the other side of the pool, screaming to the emergency operator that she was in the pool with her dying friend.

"Hurry, please! My friend is drowning and he's trying to kill me, too. Please!" Then, she held the phone up high so that Tyrese could see it, and then she pressed mute. "Come on over, and put your hands on me. Better yet," she continued as she slanted her eyes to Charlotte who was lifeless in the pool, "Jump in. You may be able to save her."

"You killed my wife? You killed Charlotte? That's your fuckin' friend, Jazz!" he shouted with all his might, in a rage as he hit his chest like he could murder Jazz without even touching her.

"And that was your wife who you told me you were leaving for me. You shouldn't give a shit, now should you?"

Tyrese never answered, and at that point, he didn't care if he was arrested or not because in his heart and mind, he knew he didn't do any of what Jazz was hollering into the phone. He only wanted Charlotte to survive.

"Oh God," he cried as he lifted her body from the water and began CPR, however, nothing happened. "Charlotte!" he yelled, but when he looked up from his wife's face, all he saw was the blood, and he wanted to draw some from Jazz with his own hands. He went in for the attack, but by that time, it was too late. As Jazz lay there on the floor, pretending to scramble for her life, it was an innocent Tyrese who was tased to the floor and finally handcuffed as the officers and emergency personnel rushed in. Jazz never stopped screaming and crying the entire time, causing them to believe she had gone into hysterics. It was only Tyrese who stared at her in disbelief, failing to defend himself, as he wondered what would be the next story she told as he was dragged away from his one true deceased love, one he would never see alive again.

**

It was three days after the murder of Charlotte Middleton that she was buried with questions coming from everywhere about her death. The media frenzy wouldn't let up, and it eventually landed right back at Trina's doorstep. A couple of bloggers even attempted to bombard her with questions about the unusual circumstances surrounding the deaths of people around her, basically poking at the fact that she was the common denominator to them all. Trina ignored the questions. Her emotions had become as rigid as brick and as hard as stone.

Although the journalist who arranged to have her interview with Evans was killed, she still wanted to know the answer to what they set out to find. Each night that went by, she felt Evans was still winning, even though he had nothing to do with Charlotte's death. It was the same scenario – whenever her life began to come back together, something prevented it from happening. She didn't want that anymore. She finally wanted to fight. It was then that she knew she would make a call and confirm the sit down with Evans despite the odds. When she did, she got the confirmation she was waiting on, and she took it. It was three days after the date of Charlotte's burial that she sat face to face with her stalker, the man that killed her husband and newborn child.

The room was cold as she sat there awaiting the arrival of the man she thought of as the most deliberate form of evil on earth. She thought back to when she first spoke to him and shuddered, and by the time her thought ended, he was there, standing at the doorway about to be led inside.

Dr. Cranizi had already warned her about the man she'd already encountered in a far more vicious way than he ever had, and it was only when Trina stared back at him blankly that he knew he was wasting his breath. There was one thing Trina knew about Evans more than he did, and that was the killer. Dr. Cranizi had only met the psycho, but never the killer side. Therefore as Mr. Stephen Evans was bound and walked inside to sit, Dr. Cranizi never took his eyes off of him for one second...nor did Trina.

"You mourn?" he asked as soon as he took a seat, however, Trina didn't answer. Her blood was boiling, and she needed to calm down. The last thing she wanted to do was satisfy him with her tears and anguish. "She's dead. I know," he stated referring to Charlotte Middleton. "Yet you still come to see me. That can only mean one thing."

"It means that I love you and I forgive you," she stated slowly and very deliberate in nature. She remembered that those words of affection was what he wanted, according to Charlotte, so she had to hold up that part of the deal. Besides, they were just words to her at that point. She could literally jump up and snap his neck in two while singing the words I love you in a song, and it wouldn't change her feelings toward him whatsoever. She would always hate him. Always.

"Does it mean that? Really, Trina?" he asked, hopeful yet not ignorantly. "Then why haven't you come and see me after all that we've been through together. I made us such a deep connection, didn't I? You can't think of them without thinking of me, now can you?"

Trina didn't budge, so Evans leaned forward and spoke again. "Hurt lives in the same place as happiness. Loneliness lives in the same place as love. I'm sure you know that by now, so," he continued in a whisper. "Wherever they are, I am as well."

"Where is he, Evans?"

"He who?" he asked as he remained leaned forward over the table.

"Creed."

"That wasn't the deal, Trina. The deal was that I would only tell Mrs. Middleton," he said staring Trina directly in the eyes. "But now that she's dead..."

"Fuck you!" Trina screamed, hauling off to slap him directly in his face. "Fuck you!" Then, she spit directly on the side of his face as the guards pulled her from the room while Evans laughed hysterically.

"Bring her back, please. I have to tell her something."

"Let me go!"

Dr. Cranizi burst through the doorway, and forced the guards to unhand Trina. Then, he convinced her to get the information that she came for because there would never be another time, especially due to the fact that she nearly struck his patient, no matter how evil he was.

"And how do you know I want another time?" she whispered, barely able to contain her rage.

"Look at yourself. It means just that much to you." He waited patiently and then gave her the extra strength with the words he said next, "Calm down and keep going." Then he whispered something in her ear. "He did that to throw you off. Don't let him win again."

The doctor then held his hands out as an inviting gesture so that she could place them inside his. Then, he began a slow but silent countdown. In about five minutes, she was ready again and was seated back in front of her stalker. As soon as she took a seat, Evans smiled.

"Back? Let me guess, Dr. Cranizi gave you a push."

She sat and waited. She was shocked at what came from his mouth next.

"He's at the overpass near your house. That's where I put him. I was already in his car. He drove, and when he drove right there at the turn, I suffocated him. I let his seat back as I strangled the life from him while people drove by. They had no idea. Then, I simply dragged him out and dropped him about ten feet down into the hole I dug by the water. Then, I walked down, pushed the dirt back over him, and came back…to you. It seemed like a place where he would truly get the rest he needed…without anyone finding him, you know."

The overpass. Trina knew exactly where he was speaking of, and it was there that no one even looked. It was just off the side of the road where extremely high weeds and brush grew, but hardly anyone cut the area. That was why no one ever found Creed's body. There was no one who suspected that his body would have been so close yet so far away.

Trina stood up and began walking away without saying a word. As she walked by him, Evans suddenly jolted himself from his seat, aiming head first for her body with his mouth wide open, hoping to taste a piece of the woman he so desired. Losing her balance, she fell to the side and hit the floor hard as the medical personnel rushed the scene while Dr. Cranizi quickly lifted her from his patient.

Evans was raised from the floor, and as he came face to face once again with Trina, he laughed. "You're gonna wish you never found him, Trina. You're gonna wish you left him decay right where he is," he called as they dragged him out of the room.

"Thank you, Dr. Cranizi. I didn't see him," she stated, quite shaken.

"But you got what you came for, and you never have to look back."

Trina stood before him with tears about to fall, but he stopped her.

"Young lady, you never have to look back again. Go properly, end that part of your life and start again. He is over. He'll be here for the rest of his life. I don't plan on setting him free willingly."

Those words brought the tears streaming down her cheeks as she thought about all she'd been through, even before she married Creed. She did have to end it. After all this time, she needed closure, and that was exactly what she got when she chose to go to locate Creed alone.

As she drove to the overpass, she parked her car further down the road. Trembling with fear and sorrow while being swallowed up by the desire to call the police prior to placing herself on such an cold case, she proceed to exit her car anyway. Her chest began to thump and her facial expression could no longer pretend she was strong enough to face those odds as she walked down the slopped decline at the overpass. She looked around but saw nothing with the naked eye as she leveled herself on the ground. It was then that she glanced down slowly at her feet. Tears began gushing out as her weeping intensified while her mind battled, wondering if she stood atop her murdered husband.

Her position was directly below where, if something were to drop, it would hit on the ground where she stood. The only other option was on the other side of the overpass. Slowly, Trina began to move the soft and slightly muddied dirt, along with the weeds and grass that covered the area, underneath her feet. Unafraid of the potential harm that could come her way as far as snakes, alligators and more, she finally fell to her knees and began digging, ripping the grass away with her bare hands.

The more she tore away, the more she was able to bury the fear that plagued her about one day having to view Creed's body. Each time her fingers touched something slightly hard, she froze, but the longer she dug, she started to pretend that it was Creed. The dirt felt like mush in her hands as she also used her knees and legs to move the mud behind her. Still, despite her digging, she uncovered nothing. As she moved further underneath the overpass to continue digging, she saw something that stood out from the rest of the mud, causing her to fall backwards and examine it intently.

The pounding of her heart began to overpower her body as it created the worst tremors she'd ever had in her lifetime, and as she stared, her body started to move toward that which she'd dug up. It was there, there in a shallow grave that appeared as if it had never fully settled down, like the earth continued to regurgitate what it didn't want…Creed's body.

"Oh God," she choked. Her hands fell deeply into the mud as she rocked back and forth, her body leaning in to see the sight she truly never wanted to see in her life. "Oh, Jesus, help me, God!" She began to rake the dirt from the surface of his body, and as she slid her hand across what was his stomach, she hit his left hand. There on his hand was his wedding ring.

From there she screamed, and she continued to scream there on her knees, crying atop the dead husband she lost on the same day her baby was killed, until the police showed up to wrench her away from the scene. Finally, through all her emotional pain, she was able to rest on earth in peace, being able to finally lay him to rest.

One Month Later

"Man, I told you. I didn't do it. She did it. Now they can't find her ass. I missed my wife's funeral, and I can't even go there without scoping out the place first because her family wants to kill me. Me! I'd never hurt Charlotte, ever. I did some bad stuff behind her back, but if I could take it all back…and Jazz, man. They don't even know where the hell she is. Lemme call you back. Tired of talking about all this." He hung up the phone frustrated, holding back his tears yet again as a façade as his depression worsened.

Tyrese was set free from jail after there were holes in Jazz's story that the police decided needed further investigating. Upon further investigation, Tyrese was found not guilty due to a snag in Jazz's story versus Tyrese's that same week of his arrest. According to Jazz the two never had an affair, however, when Tyrese was questioned, he referred them to the very last date they were together in a hotel. From there, they investigated and pulled the footage from that day, and there it was…he and Jazz… going inside the hotel room, kissing and holding hands. It was that atop the handwriting from the various notes left by Jazz. They all matched. The same person who killed Patrice also killed Charlotte, and the police were able to make that proven based on a positive match for Jazz's handwriting where she worked.

Unfortunately, before they could bring Jazz back into the station, she'd vanished, knowing that they were on to her. It had been exactly thirty days since her disappearance, and absolutely no one had a clue where she'd gone. She was a wanted woman.

Charlotte's picture remained on the nightstand while a portrait of them both, when they married, hung proudly in the hallway. However, although he enjoyed looking at it as a reminder of the loving wife he once had, he felt a tremendous amount of guilt behind knowing that she would still be alive if it wasn't for his cheating ways. Despite the charges against him being dropped, he still felt like he was in a prison, unable to even visit her grave in peace. The truth was that he'd never been to the site of her burial at all. He would only sit in the car and stare, occasionally get out and stand at the road and look, however, he never made the trek to her plot.

"I'm coming, Charlotte. I'll be there." He picked up his car keys and without changing out of his dingy jeans and shirt, he finally decided to do that something that needed to be done. Laying all the guilt aside and wanting to be a better man about everything in his life, no matter what, he needed to face what he knew he did, regardless of if he wasn't the one committing the actual crime. The one he needed to make peace with was God first and then Charlotte because it was them who he betrayed for his own selfish pleasure, costing the life of his wife thus his own in a sense.

With tears in his eyes, he tried again to leave the house and go to the cemetery to make his peace, but he fell back onto the bed, unable to even make it to the room door. It was there that he lay until he fell asleep once again for hours as the sun set. By the time he woke up, it was in the middle of the night, and all his dreams were about his deceased wife.

Salty white lines from tears lined his face, and his eyes felt like they were glued shut from mucus. He wiped his face with his hands and immediately smelled a scent that he hadn't smelled since he last saw his wife. It was her perfume.

Sitting up startled in the bed, he located the bottle on the dresser where Charlotte kept it at all times. It hadn't been moved, and yet, the scent was strong. It was all over the sheets as he lifted them to smell her, and as he rushed onto his feet, he began to smile, convincing himself that her death was all one big nightmare.

"Charlotte!" he called loudly. "Charlotte," he yelled once again as he searched the fragrant room and then the dark hallway. He rushed into the living room and flicked on the light where the smell of her perfume was literally on everything. Turning around in circles, he began to feel lost as he didn't see her anywhere. His sobbing increased as he lost all hope, despite the strong scent. "Please don't be dead. Please, let me see you again, please, baby," he moaned as he flicked on the hallway light, his head hanging low and confused.

As he dragged his feet against the floor and his body against the wall, he finally looked up at the beautiful portrait hanging of them at the end of the hallway from their wedding day. He stalled as the portrait didn't look the same. There was a large slice running across it from one corner to the next.

Without a second thought, he rushed the portrait, desperately hurt at the sight of it, and rubbed his hand across the large gash in an attempt to put it back together perfectly. However, he stopped his patchwork when he saw her from the side of his eye. She was sitting on his bed, pointing a pistol directly at him.

He stumbled over his own feet to face her and called her name aloud. "Jazz?"

"I'll never leave you lonely, baby."

The gun fired after she turned it on herself. He watched as her body fell atop the mattress dead. Tyrese, then, dropped to his knees in silence, stuck listening to his own voice on a recorder that she held in her lifeless hand repeating the same phrase continuously.

"I love you, Jazz. I love you, Jazz. I love you…"

His torment continues.

THE END

For more stories, visit mirikacornelius.com.

Thank you.

Enjoyed? Please leave a review and turn the page to see more books from which to choose!

More Akirim Press Books

(akirimpress.com)

Books by Mirika Mayo Cornelius

(mirikacornelius.com)

Secret

Colored Lily: Poppa Took My Innocence

Paton

The Secret Novel Collection

Ain't Quite What I Thought!

Ain't Quite What I Thought! 2

First Degree Sins

Cold Blooded Goons

Inside the Gates of Doons

Sunny Sides of My Shade

Murders at Gabriel's Trails: The Complete 5 Part Series

Sins of Bain

Deception at Gabriel's Trails

I Thought I Was Alone

I Thought I Was Alone 2

I Thought I Was Alone 3

Most Wanted Felon

Curse the Cotton

Disguised by a Raging Smile

Books by Rod Cornelius

(rodcornelius.com)

Ugly

Single Again

Diggin' Gold

The Trusted

Ghetto Eyes

The Best Kept Secrets

Whatever It Takes

When It Comes Around

Books by Cyan Deane

(mirikacornelius.com/cyan-deane)

Dead Man's Mayhem

Execution's Karma

www.ingramcontent.com/pod-product-compliance
Lightning Source LLC
Chambersburg PA
CBHW071040250626
47159CB00012B/1337